RISE OF THE SONS

Sons of the Phoenix: Book 3

A novel by

JOSEPH MACKAY

Rise of the Sons
Part Three
Sons of the Phoenix
Copyright © 2017 by Joseph Mackay
ISBN: 978-0-9981321-2-9

Cover Design by Whendell Digital Art, whendell.deviantart.com
Edited by Kristina Circelli, www.kristinacircelli.com

To Connor and Alex
And to the Moonlight that lit the way
You are my inspiration

RISE OF THE SONS

Sons of the Phoenix: Book 3

PROLOGUE

THE WORLD HAD CHANGED.

In 2051, mankind had drained the earth of its fossil fuels. For years, humanity's best scientists looked for alternative forms of energy to help sustain life on earth. Many technologies were created, but all were insufficient to satisfy man's rate of consumption.

In 2074, a team of oceanic explorers uncovered the wreckage of an alien vessel at the bottom of the Pacific Ocean. Among the early discoveries made while studying the ship was slipstream drive technology. This technology gave man the ability to increase particles faster than light, allowing the creation and stabilization of wormholes. It wasn't long after that humanity discovered a way to follow the particles through the folds in space-time.

Probes were sent out at first and, soon after, manned exploratory flights, searching for habitable planets and other viable resources. In 2095, the first colony vessels were sent through slipstream folds to various star systems to establish livable conditions on habitable planets and report on the level of available resources. Most colonies performed their function as best they could with limited interaction with the United Earth Defense Force (UEDF), the collaboration of earth's nations and governments.

Soon the majority of the population of Earth became complacent, satisfied to let the global government use these worlds to help sustain human life.

For nearly forty years the Earth Military Council (EMC) of

the United Earth Defense Force studied the alien vessel to learn what other secrets it possessed. They raised it from the ocean floor through a feat of engineering and moved it to a secret location on the island of Kita-Daito, near Japan. However, none of their efforts allowed them access to the inside of the ship, until they discovered the device.

They called it OMBI, the Omni-Manifold Bracer Implant, which, by connecting to the dominant arm of its host, allowed for the free exchange of binary data and human thought. The first tests resulted in a mental overload of information, causing the brain to shut down, killing the host. Inhibitor chips were designed and added to the OMBI, but the operators still suffered from brain malfunctions and ultimately ended up going insane after a few days of use.

It was by accident that a researcher discovered the device performed better when used by a child. Children, with their developing brains, had proven more successful in binding with the synapse-sync technologies. Fusing their brain functions with operating computers allowed them to experience combat, piloting, and operating functions at the speed of thought.

In need of viable hosts for the OMBI devices and sensing the unrest of the population of earth, the Earth Military Council (EMC), under the leadership of General Harruhama, staged an attack on the colonies under the guise of an alien threat. The "Gortha" were invented by the EMC and blamed for the attack. They were characterized by Earth's media as an evil race of lizard-like humanoids with superior technology and a hunger for planetary resources. In 2115, in response to the Gortha threat, the UEDF was taken over by the EMC, putting General Harruhama in charge as a global dictator.

The people lived in fear of humanity's new enemy, getting sporadic media reports from the front lines of the battle, mankind's colonies.

Under the guise of needing better resources to battle the Gortha threat, the EMC opened the "OMBIcademy" within the halls of the alien vessel. Children were drafted into military service for their ability to safely connect with the OMBI technology, in order to facilitate the unlocking of the ship's mysteries.

Humanity was all too willing to offer its brightest children to their government to protect the human race, all in the name of the greater good.

CHAPTER 1

Tomorrow, I'll be Dead

THE CADENCE OF RAIN TAPPED ITS MELANCHOLY SONG in Healdsburg, California on the morning of March 16th, 2121, giving the pavement of the long drive up the Mercer estate a rich, musty scent. William Mercer had loved that smell ever since he was a child. He always took time to consciously slow down and appreciate how simply pleasing it was to him. Today he was inhaling the petrichor as if it were the first and last time he'd ever get to.

"It just might be," he muttered from under his full-faced helmet.

The soft rumble of the engine of his Triumph Bonneville echoed through the maze of sculptures he had collected; heroic figures, eternally holding their stoic poses, lining the drive to the Mercer Estate.

"His collection is the most grandiose monument to the man's hubris to ever be compiled," William smirked, quoting a ten-year-old article. The author had been offended apparently, and even after all this time it still made William laugh.

On that particular morning he nodded to each of them as he passed them, a quiet salute to his sentries as they stood in defiance of the storm.

Returning after a six-day, twelve-hundred-mile ride had

William feeling sore, cold, and tired. His muscles ached as he dismounted his bike in the workshop and headed into the house. Six stressful days, traveling up and down the California coast in an attempt to learn the truth about the Incident of 2115. What the media had heralded as an alien invasion, resulting in the death of his wife, Captain Marlena Mercer, turned out to be a false flag attack. A betrayal against his wife for the Earth Military Council to seize power.

He had found the truth he was looking for in San Diego at the burned-out residence of one of the former crew members of the Andromeda, the ship that had been rescued by Marlena during the attack. An old groundskeeper had informed him that the ship had never returned and had, in fact, arrived at its destination of Aeris VII in the Hourglass Nebula after being betrayed by the United Earth Defense Force.

White-hot rage fueled thoughts of revenge, the storm doing nothing to dampen the fury he felt. In the back of his mind he knew that he had to protect his two adopted sons, who were being trained as soldiers at the UEDF-controlled OMBIcademy. It was that thought, along with the recklessness of anger, that gave birth to his plan.

He worked tirelessly for two days, without a break and without sleep. The first day he spent reinforcing the survival shelter he had built under the house. On the second he began compounding homemade explosives. The instructions were easy enough to find in the books of his extensive library. He used the estate's own gas lines as his primary source of fuel. He didn't think much about destroying the home that he had built with his family; he became a man of a singular purpose.

By the morning of March 18th, 2121 the rain had finally stopped. After a hot shower and one last check of his gear, William Mercer sat down at his desk. He took a deep breath, mentally preparing himself. He barely found the strength but finally opened a folder on his computer that he had never thought he would open again, a family vacation from 2114.

The photos popped up on the screen and began the slide-show. The first one set the tone, a cabin at the foot of a mountain range, a lone wisp of smoke rising into the sky. The second stole his breath, Marlena standing atop a hill smiling back at him, her dark hair dancing like fire from the wind against the background of green rolling hills and a cloudless blue sky.

Tears rimmed his dark-blue eyes as he looked at her. The slideshow took the image away and flashed through several of Alex and Connor driving, shooting, and hiking about. William smiled in defiance of the empty feeling in his chest. More pictures of Marlena appeared.

William took a deep, deliberate breath and closed his eyes. He let himself remember how it felt have his wife in his arms, the sweet smell of her hair as he breathed in, the warmth of her body pressed against his. In his mind he felt himself brush her cheek with his fingers and then press his lips against hers. For that moment, William Mercer felt at peace.

In the next, reality then came crashing down like a bolt of lightning. He quickly closed the pictures and moved his cursor over a dangerous icon, one that he knew he would not be able to access. The Andromeda black box video. He took one more steadying breath.

"Looks like tomorrow I'll be dead," he whispered to the empty room.

Click.

—

He sat in his office for the remainder of the day watching ho-lotube reports about the destruction of Black Squadron at the hands of the Gortha. William held no hope that he would ever see his stepson, Alex, alive again, and in those few moments renewed despair ravaged his core. Nearly broken, he knew that he had no options left and only a single straight path lay before him, the path of retribution.

The man had absolutely nothing to lose, and when he heard the footsteps outside of the door to the office, a sinister grin formed upon his lips. He struck a solitary key on his datapad before setting it down.

"Surely an architect is not so dangerous that the EMC would have to send an assassin," William proclaimed.

"Surely an architect with such keen senses may be more than an architect," a voice quipped from the other side of the door.

"I'm unarmed. You can come in, the EMC has taken everything from me now, except my life. But I suspect that you're here to remedy that problem."

The words were intended as a ruse; however, the sincere hopelessness behind them threatened to overwhelm him.

The door creaked open slowly and a plain-looking man walked in. His eyes darted from side to side then settled upon William. The operative's dark armor was almost imperceptible beneath his clothing and William couldn't make out any weapons. Everything about him seemed nonchalant except his eyes, which betrayed his experience.

"Just one? I'm offended," William scoffed.

"I have an entire squad already inside, you should be flattered. Apparently someone thought highly enough of you to send me with backup. But looking at you, maybe I should be the one who is offended."

"Touché," William smirked.

"This can either be painless or it can hurt. It's up to you, Mr. Mercer." The operative grinned, setting a white capsule on the desk.

William paused a moment then looked from the vial to the

man and said, "I have heard that operatives are rare and highly trained."

The man bit. "Indeed, there are only three of my class in the entire EMC. But I digress, what will it be?"

"Right to the point, very well, I choose pain. But before you proceed, I have something to share with you."

The operative grinned as he cocked his head curiously.

"What could you possibly have to share that you think I would even be remotely interested in?"

"This!"

William placed a datapad on the desk, which displayed a timer reading fifteen seconds, and was counting down.

"You should really learn to notice when someone is stalling," he said, stealing the operative's grin.

In one fluid motion the operative pulled a gun from his sleeve and pointed it at William's head.

"Shut it down," the operative demanded.

William burst into laughter.

"Sorry, no off switch on this one," William laughed.

The operative cocked back the hammer and took a step forward. William began to laugh so hard that he fell out of his chair.

The operative turned to run, leaving William exactly where he wanted to be.

He grabbed his datapad and counted off the remaining seconds as he opened a hidden panel behind his bookshelf that opened into a concrete stairway. He leapt down a short flight of stairs and through an open doorway, slamming it shut behind him.

He wasn't entirely sure that he would survive the blast even in his shelter but, somewhere in the back of his mind, a macabre thought formed as he sealed the door. His story would not end with so little blood.

The explosion rocked the fertile valley of the Russian river.

The statues of carved stone gave way and burst apart, causing stone to rain down for miles around. The glorious tribute to the heart of man's greatness was gone in the blink of an eye, engulfed in the flame of retribution.

—

William awoke with a start in the cold, predawn hours of August 15th, 2121. He wasn't sure why he had dreamed about the day he had become an outlaw but, looking around at the smoldering devastation of a war torn San Francisco, he began to wonder if it had been worth it. Gathering himself, he listened carefully as the wind howled through the skeleton of what was left of the ruined building he had spent the night in.

No sounds of any immediate threat.

He took a deep breath; the stench of death lingered in the stagnant morning air. William stretched his aching body out one limb at a time, his joints groaning like an old ship. The throbbing in his ankle reminded him that he had broken it nearly a month before.

He forced himself out of the warmth of his bedroll and looked out the remains of a nearby window. The sun had not yet risen, but the sky had taken on a maroon color and William forced another deep breath, which caused him to wince.

"Still not quite healed," he muttered to himself as he examined the wound in his side where his lung had been punctured.

The cold made the pain worse so he cut his stretching routine short and built a small fire. It took a few minutes to get going, but once he warmed up, he gathered his gear. Examining the mechanized battle armor as he dressed, his fingers testing the patch job where the armor had been punctured.

It was the armor that had once belonged to the UEDF Operative who had been sent to kill him. It had survived an explosion, fire, a motorcycle crash, countless bullets, and finally tore a bit when he had crashed a transport into a battle suit.

William smiled as put on the suit, feeling the familiar strength returning to his body.

"At this point, I wonder how far I could even walk without you," he remarked offhandedly.

A sound from the street below caused William to tense up. He instinctively grabbed his three-barreled shotgun and moved to the window. He spotted the stray cat as it darted out of a fallen trash can and let out a sigh of relief.

The UEDF troops in the area had been organizing a grid search in an attempt to corner him and his stepson, giving them little time to rest. William had been unable to relax for days.

From the next room of the apartment he could hear Alex softly snoring through the ruckus outside. The kid had finally slept since the two had reunited and William wasn't about to take that from him.

Quietly collecting his gear, William took an unsteady step toward the door. Moving quietly took effort, but he

crept into the hall, down the stairwell, and out onto the street.

—

Captain Alex Pereira, known as Mephisto to his former squadron, awoke long after the sun had risen. With the sunlight glittering off San Francisco bay, he got his first good look at the structure around him. His olive-green eyes went wide as he ran his fingers through the mop of brown hair that had been growing out on his head.

"How is this place even standing?" he muttered in disbelief as he sat up.

More than half of the structure was gone and several holes

were so wide he could fly Skoll through them without touching the sides.

"I can't believe I let you talk me into staying here," Alex remarked before he realized he was alone.

"It will hold. Trust me. I built it," he continued, candidly mimicking William's voice.

The boy laughed despite himself as he stretched his sore body. He had been enjoying his reunion with his stepfather more than he expected to, given the circumstances.

He hopped to his feet in one fluid motion, mentally activating his OMBI functions. *Motion Sensor. Thermal.*

"No threats," he mused. "No William?"

He reached out through his OMBI, feeling the area. He furrowed his brow in frustration that so few of the many cameras in the city were operational. Shrugging, he pushed his thoughts farther, to the waters beyond Breaker Beach where he had crashed Skoll. He let himself feel it beneath the waves, slowly absorbing minerals from the sand.

"Almost ready, I guess," he lamented, uncertainly. "I'm going to need you soon."

Somewhere in the city, Alex's former friend Austin Hughes, who was called Vertigo in Black Squadron, along with several thousand UEDF troops, were hunting for him. Alex had been able to disable Austin's vessel, Fenris, temporarily. But he knew it would only be a matter of time before he would face him again.

He tried to sense Fenris to no avail.

Alex was deep in thought when he heard the steps of familiar boots.

"Did I wake you?" William asked quietly.

Even his softly spoken words seemed to echo in the eerie calm remains of the once-great city.

"No, I've been awake for a while," Alex whispered, "and my motion sensor picked you up two blocks away."

William smirked as he set down the supplies. Moving to check on the fire, he stoked it back to life, adding more wood from a broken table.

"Chocolate chip pancakes?" William raised a soot-covered eyebrow.

"Where did you find...? Never mind, yes!" Alex blurted, smiling. For a moment he felt like a kid again, having breakfast before school. The moment passed as he added, "You didn't steal that stuff, did you?"

William shrugged as he set up the kitchen and began mixing the batter. "Would you believe me if I said that I left money in the store I got this from?"

Alex grinned. He was sure that William did leave money for the food, even though it was an empty gesture in a city on the edge of total destruction. A quiet minute passed before Alex spoke again.

"Mom doesn't look any different," he stated suddenly, causing William to freeze. "She's been slipstreaming around to lead the rebellion in the colonies so much that she's only aged like, three years."

William looked down at the stove, smiling as he imaged her face.

"You know. Her face is still the first thing I see every time I close my eyes," William mused. "How long were you with her?"

"We spent a couple months together on Aeris VII. William, you would love her house, it's a lot like home. Heck, you'd love that entire city. They modeled all their architecture based on your work."

"I can't wait to see it," William beamed. "I'm trying to imagine it."

"So it's on the edge of this huge lake and..." Alex babbled.

The moment was interrupted as a distant explosion caused them both to go silent. They both tensed up, listening carefully.

Without another word, William finished making breakfast. They ate quickly and packed up their supplies.

"William, you never asked me how I crash landed on Earth," Alex said as they were almost done.

"When did we have time?"

"I know. But it's important. Mom and I slipstreamed here to get ahead of a battle group that had attacked us on Aeris. We were ambushed by Harruhama, Fenris, and another ship that is a lot like mine."

William listened intently as Alex seemed to struggle for the right words.

"Connor was the pilot of that ship. I'm not sure what they did to him, but he got hurt, bad. Just before I put him and Mom through a slipstream back to Aeris, her comms got cut off and I don't know what happened to her."

William's face went white as Alex spoke.

"I'm worried about them, William, but until Skoll has finished repairing himself there isn't anything we can do. Sorry to tell you like this," Alex finished.

William's tension diminished slightly as he shook his head.

"It's not your fault, Alex. Thank you for telling me. Maybe we can contact them somehow..."

"I thought of that, but they will be in the slipstream for another week at least."

William was nodding before he was done.

"We need to get out of this city and get somewhere that we can make contact when they do."

"I was thinking the same thing. We can use Skoll soon, but there are a lot of UEDF troops between us and the beach. Fenris too..." Alex trailed off.

"There is also something else we need to worry about," William said as they began to head down the stairs. "When I was in New York, the UEDF fired on the city from orbit to try to kill me. I wouldn't be surprised if they tried that again, especially now that the two of us are together."

"So they just decided to destroy a whole city to kill you?" Alex asked as they arrived on the street. "I guess you've been busy."

William chuckled at that, despite himself. He suddenly looked a lot older than Alex remembered him.

"Maybe we need to show these clowns just who they're up against," Alex quipped, smiling at his stepfather.

The smile was infectious and soon William was smiling too.

They had covered almost half a block when Alex stopped suddenly, turning his head sharply northward and closing his eyes.

"What is it?" William asked quietly, reaching for his weapon.

"I think Skoll is ready. I'm not sure how I know that, but if I can get to him, I think we can get out of the city today," Alex stated.

"It's still a long way, we better get moving."

Alex was nodding before William had finished his sentence and the two turned northward and began to pick their way through the rubble.

—

A few miles away in the Presidio, Vertigo was attempting to remove the locks Alex had placed on his systems a week before. During the attack, just before defeating Alex, he had been struck by an allied aircraft and was subsequently disabled by his cunning, former captain. He still wasn't exactly sure how Fenris had been disabled or what the connection between Alex and the rebels was, but he was getting close to solving the riddle before him.

The lockout of his vessel came in the form of several puzzles that, at first, had baffled Vertigo to the point of almost giving up on his ship. After a couple days of splitting his time between organizing a manhunt with UEDF command in orbit and trying to reconnect with his ship, he discovered a pattern and had managed to solve some of the easier locks.

The most recent puzzle he had been stuck on manifested a three-dimensional maze that continued to change as he progressed through it. There were no exits, as the goal wasn't escape, but rather to discover what was at a middle he couldn't seem to find.

Although it had taken several days, Vertigo finally managed to find the way. The trick had been to use the answers to the riddle locks as passwords to move through walls before the maze had changed too much. He beamed as he finished it. His smile became a frown when he realized that there was no one to celebrate his victory with.

As Fenris began to stand, Vertigo marveled at its form. The battle suit stood thirty feet high and, with a broad chest, looked vaguely humanoid other than its terrifying wolf face.

"Hello again," he grinned, feeling the connection return through his OMBI.

As if in response, Fenris howled.

CHAPTER 2

Raining Fire

THE COLD MORNING WIND BLEW A LOOSE STRAND OF hair from his face as Arthur Zendt moved with his men quietly among the buildings in what was left of China town. His one-hundred eager rebels had become seventy-two weary veterans over the course of the week as the large-scale engagements devolved into smaller skirmishes, leaving the city in tatters.

Zendt, a lean man of just twenty-two, wore a fresh gash over his left eye from landing wrong in a debris pile as he took cover the day before. He was also fairly sure that his shoulder was partially dislocated, as it made a painful clicking sound as he raised his left arm to signal his men to stop.

Grimacing through the pain, he took a deep breath and strained his ears for the sound he had thought he heard a moment before.

Holding up two fingers, he motioned for his scouts to proceed while the bulk of his force held their positions.

He watched his scouts from behind a pile of rubble as they carefully entered the apartment building ahead.

"Be clear," he whispered to himself, "please be clear."

He brushed the dark hair from his eyes and gripped the rifle he had picked off a fallen UEDF soldier. Out of the corner of his eyes he could see his men shifting anxiously.

Nearly two minutes had passed and Zendt was about to give the order to advance when a low hum cut the silence. It quickly grew into a rumble until the rubble on the street began to rattle.

"Fall back!" shouted one of the scouts as he burst from the apartment building onto the street at a dead run.

The men immediately began their retreat, stumbling over debris as they ran. They hadn't gotten far before the walls of the gray building burst apart, revealing a thirty-foot-tall bipedal mechanical wolf. Debris showered the men, crushing some, disorienting others.

The wolf straightened slowly, impassively surveying Zendt's forces.

The roar of machinegun fire broke the tension.

"Run!" Zendt screamed. "Cease fire!"

The rhythmic whistle of bullets ricocheting off metal drowned out Zendt's orders. The rockets came next, shaking the street with explosions and fire as they slammed into the monstrosity.

Through it all, the wolf didn't move.

—

Inside Fenris, Vertigo scanned the assailants one by one, looking for his former commander. When he was confident that none of the men in front of him had an OMBI, he sent a message to UEDF command.

To: UEDF Command

Subject: -

Message: VIP target not in group 7, orders?

Vertigo didn't have to wait long.

—*Message Received*—

"Eliminate all targets and continue searching."

Delivered 10:18 2121-03-16

From: UEDF Command

The boy frowned.

"An order is an order," he sighed as he manifested a chain-gun in the powerful hands of his ship.

"Run, idiots," he murmured as the barrel began to spin.

The men almost all stopped attacking just before the barrage shredded the vehicles on the street and the buildings beyond. Men dove behind cover that was quickly destroyed until the entire street was nearly entirely ground to dust.

The battle was over quickly. A follow up scan from his OMBI confirmed: *seventy-two causalities.*

Vertigo shut his eyes and forced away the thought.

"I better get moving," he said after a few moments.

As the day continued, killing got easier. He found more groups of rebels using his OMBI's motion sensor. Coordinating with the UEDF ground troops, he effectively continued destroying them and the building they hid in, leaving fewer places for Alex to run.

⁓

Several blocks away, on a hill looking down toward China Town and the bay beyond, Alex watched as the UEDF troops rallied behind the battle suit vessel, destroying entire blocks in their wake.

"I think they're after us, you see the pattern that they are using to search? It's pretty efficient," William said, walking up beside him as a building collapsed in a puff of gray smoke.

"Yeah, I see it. If I can get to my ship, we can stop this," Alex repeated, turning his head and raising his chin to the northeast.

"And how far are we away now?" William smirked expectantly.

"Mile and a half or so," came the predictable reply. "Sorry, I know that's annoying. He's calling to me though. He knows I need him."

A frown crossed William's face and eventually devolved into a smile.

"There are a lot of enemy troops between here and there. You need a diversion, something to draw that ship's attention."

Alex was shaking his head before William finished speaking.

"The last diversion I had fighting him literally killed you. Also, I am pretty sure that I can't trick him like I did before, even if we could hit him hard enough to distract him. He isn't stupid," Alex explained, pointing toward Fenris, which was lifting higher into the air.

William studied the scene as the wolf began flying back and forth, scanning the city below. "If we do nothing, we're dead in a matter of hours. How fast can you get to your ship if you had to?"

Alex looked northward again through the rubble of the devastated city and closed his eyes.

"By air, maybe thirty seconds, but I'd be seen and probably shot down before I made it. By ground, a little over a minute if there aren't too many obstacles, a little longer if I have to swim. By foot, about nine minutes?" Alex finished uncertainly.

William only nodded as Alex spoke. He took his gaze from Fenris and began scanning the area around him. Not far away he noticed an undisturbed entrance to an underground parking structure that appeared to be intact despite the destroyed building leaning on top of it.

"By ground it is. I'll buy you the time. But, come back and help me as quickly as you can," William adding, grinning.

Alex pursed his lips, the reluctance clear in his eyes.

"Wait here a second," William said as he ran across the street, disappearing into the garage.

Alex began to mentally search his OMBI menu for the best way to get to the beach.

"Terrain is encumbered. Speed necessary. What to choose?" he mumbled to himself.

He settled on motocross bike. Eying the distance and turning back to the sound of gunfire in the south, Alex steeled himself for the fight to come.

William emerged a few moments later rolling out a newer-looking sport bike to the entrance and waved Alex over.

"Can that help me start this?" William asked, nodding to Alex's OMBI.

On cue, the motorcycle's electric engine started as Alex shrugged. The older man mounted the vehicle and nodded as Alex began manifesting his own motorcycle, facing northward.

"Ride safe," William offered, placing his hand on Alex's shoulder.

"You too." Alex nodded.

They started off in opposite directions, picking up speed until William was off Alex's motion sensor entirely.

He was worried. As good as he was, William wouldn't last long against Fenris, and Alex knew that he would have to hurry if he wanted to see his stepfather alive again.

"Ride hard. Ride fast," Alex muttered to himself as he accelerated. The dilapidated buildings zipped by as Alex maneuvered around old cars until he came to a small hill of rubble. He sped up it, launching himself into the air and landing on the other side right in the middle of a UEDF patrol.

Not taking the subtle approach, William sped straight toward Fenris. He pulled the shotgun off his shoulder and, using one hand, fired a barrage of explosive pellets toward the battle suit before sharply turning down a cross street, in the opposite direction from where Alex had gone.

Vertigo, true to Alex's warnings, did not waste time before launching a counter attack of chain-gun fire, which trailed behind William's motorcycle until a building obscured the line of sight.

He saw Fenris rise above the roof line in his left mirror as it came after him. The large vessel closed the distance quickly and William had to rely on quick turns and the agility of his motorcycle to avoid getting cornered.

William sped with all haste, driving at the edge of recklessness, desperately trying to avoid obstacles while keeping cover between him and the wolf. His mind was a whirlwind of lightning reactions and changing plans, relying on reflexes honed from a lifetime of riding.

"Might as well make this good!" William yelled to himself as he turned, losing sight of Fenris and heading down one of San Francisco's steeper hills, speeding up as fast as his bike would go.

It was too late when he realized his mistake. Fenris could fly and could easily cut him off. The wolf landed hard on the road ahead of him, aiming its weapons.

Going much too fast to turn, William watched as the large ship aimed the chain-gun directly at him, its barrels spinning furiously.

As if on cue, Fenris' head turned sharply northward. The ship leapt into the air, just over William's head.

"No!" William cried out, trying to control the bike as he fumbled for his shotgun.

It was too late. Vertigo had sensed the ruse and was heading directly for Alex.

As if an apparent afterthought, Fenris launched several small missiles before moving out of sight. The projectiles soared up into the air, leaving a trail of white smoke, before sharply turning and pursuing the man.

William screamed a curse as he got low on the bike, beneath the wind.

Going too fast to dodge and not fast enough to outrun the incoming missiles, William pulled the throttle as hard as he could, heading straight toward San Francisco Bay.

—

Alex knew that he had been identified by the checkpoint guards as he rode through them. He kept his course, now that only direct speed would mean the difference between success and failure. He subconsciously raised a force shield around him and the motorcycle using his OMBI. Tiny little pinpricks rippled through his mind as bullets bounced harmlessly aside, before he turned down another street.

The sound of his motor roared in his ears as he rode, the ocean quickly coming into view beyond the grassy hills of the Presidio. The once-beautiful base was mostly a smoldering ruin now, forcing him to dodge around small craters from the battle a week before.

So intent on his speed, Alex nearly ran into a blockade of UEDF soldiers who had set up a base on the site of where Alex had first met with the rebels.

"Well that's great," Alex quipped as he changed his direction toward the beach, jumping a small fence and spraying sand as he landed. "I guess they know I'm here."

He could feel Skoll in the waves below. His heart pounded

as the shared excitement of a reunion urged him on. The feeling distracted him long enough to miss the figure landing on the beach ahead. Alex let out a gasp as he finally saw it.

Fenris had come.

—

His target moved with the grace of a cat, landing on his feet in a sprint as the motorcycle he was riding faded away under him.

Alex didn't waste time in launching a few small missiles at Fenris, which Vertigo easily absorbed, refusing to even raise additional armor or shields from his OMBI.

To his credit Alex didn't let up, launching a second volley as he charged forward, shouting something that Vertigo couldn't make out through the rumble of explosions on the hull of his ship. Vertigo realized his mistake in not attacking immediately when the second volley burst into a heavy smoke screen. On instinct, he switched to the motion sensor mode of his OMBI.

Confusion immediately gripped his mind as he detected several objects moving toward him.

"What the heck?" he muttered as a missile exploded into Fenris' side.

Switching to infrared, his eyes went wide at the sight of the three hulking A-25 combat drones coming at him, their treads rattling across the sand. He manifested a rifle and blasted the first drone, destroying it easily with a shot through the power core. Grinning, he then manifested a large, two-pronged spear as he charged in to attack the other two. Two quick swipes in the strong hands of Fenris and Vertigo quickly destroyed the second drone.

Vertigo turned to face the third that was charging, full speed, straight at him. The drone's large machinegun glowed fiercely red as it flared to life with another barrage of gunfire.

Charging through, Fenris swung the spear straight down.

The drone dissipated just before the spear's impact, leaving Fenris over-extended and off balance as a rocket exploded against his back, knocked it into the sand. Vertigo turned as he got up to see Alex near the water's edge, running out into the waves.

—

Water sprayed up onto his face with each step. Alex ran through the surf as hard as he had ever run, but he knew he wouldn't make it.

Alex had barely manifested his black armor when a swing from the two-pronged spear knocked him back onto the beach. Dazed from the heavy hit, he barely managed to keep his armor active as Fenris stalked over to him. Its very steps shook the ground beneath him as he struggled to stand. The spear came down, its prongs piercing the sand on both sides of him, pinning him to the ground.

His arms were free, if he could just manifest a weapon. Nothing came to his mind that would help him. More of his focus was needed to keep his armor up with each passing second as he felt the pressure build against his chest.

"Your time has come, old friend," he heard Vertigo say in a familiar, albeit metallic, voice as the pressure of the spear began to crush his chest. He struggled for breath, fought back with his very will to survive.

Black spots began to pepper his vision. As Alex's mind begin to fade, images of his younger brother and childhood found their way into his thoughts.

Connor. Quick thinking, defiant Connor. He would have found a way. Alex coughed.

The thought took root somewhere in Alex's fading consciousness and he reached out with it through his OMBI.

Time seemed to slow down as his mind expanded into the world around him. Fenris felt like a dark wall, impenetrable and cold. In the waves beyond, Skoll felt like a bright torch that's fire was burning toward him. So close, but unreachable.

Fighting to stay conscious, Alex could feel his armor beginning to dissipate.

Then he sensed it.

It was faint and distant, but it was something he could use. He reached for it even as his mind was slipping from consciousness. He pulled with everything he had left, making the shape of a gun with his hand.

With his last breath he managed to whisper, "You lose," then he pulled the trigger.

⁓

Aboard the UEDF Paladin, the ATG Gunner of one of the ship's three main cannons was watching the battle unfold on the beach below. He had been on standby for several days, taking turns at his station, awaiting the order to level the city of San Francisco. His most recent orders had come from the surface when the target he was tracking had gotten close to a UEDF base. The message on his screen read, "Eliminate target."

His cannon was already charged when Fenris had begun its attack, so the gunner waited and watched eagerly as one kid fought off a huge battle suit vessel.

The fight was nearly over now, the kid being crushed by Fenris' spear. He was watching so intently that when his console turned red, he didn't understand. He stared unbelieving at his monitor, blinking several times to make sure he was seeing right. There was no mistake though, his cannon had fired.

—

Vertigo's sensors flared to life with a warning as the area around him began to brighten, sand rising from the beach up into the air as the gravity shifted. He let up slightly on his spear, trying to adjust for the shift.

"What's going on?" he shouted.

Orbital attack eminent.

He didn't understand. He impulsively went to his OMBI's motion sensor to scan for attackers. The mistake cost him a couple seconds and he began manifesting additional armor before he realized it.

As the moment passed, Vertigo tensed, bracing for the impact.

—

Unable to clear the blast entirely, Alex used his OMBI to raise his shield and reinforce his armor as he scrambled out from under the two-pronged spear. He only got a couple steps, moving quick through the rising sands, before diving forward onto the ground as the bombardment struck.

The blast slammed Fenris into the sand, spraying shards of newly formed glass and sand into the sky, causing the air to ignite with a rain of glittering colors. The force of the blast knocked Alex across the sandy beach and into a roll, which continued on for several seconds before Alex came to a stop, face down in the sand. His shield and armor had absorbed most of the blast before dissipating, leaving the edges of his flight suit and hair badly singed.

Alex managed his way onto uncertain feet and ran. He didn't look back and didn't slow. He ran as hard as he could to the edge of the water, trying, dizzily, to focus on stepping forward as he stumbled into the surf.

The Jet Ski materialized in front of him as he selected the first motorized watercraft on his mental OMBI menu. In one unsteady motion, Alex climbed on and splashed through the breakers, speeding forward to where his ship awaited him.

He finally glanced back to see Fenris nearly on its feet as Alex let the Jet Ski dissipate. The vehicle disappearing beneath him and Alex dove into the water above Skoll.

—

Vertigo shrugged off the disorientation as quickly as he could. The blast had hurt and he could feel that Fenris had suffered some damage. He bit back his frustration and forced his heavy ship out over the water toward where Alex had dove in.

Using his OMBI's motion sensor, he watched as the movement changed from small object into larger object. Moments later, the figure of a black, dragon-faced samurai burst from the waves, spraying a rainbow of mist into the sky, its eyes shining fiercely with a pale-green light.

Vertigo grabbed the sides of his head as it rippled with pain when he looked directly at Skoll before its figure distorted into that of a Gortha fighter.

The Gortha ship moved more quickly than Vertigo remembered that it could, striking Fenris head on with a pair of whips made up of interlinking metal blades. Before he could bring up Fenris' armor again, the weight of the slashing whips slammed into him, knocking him off balance.

He knew he was outmatched. Damaged and losing momentum quickly, Vertigo maneuvered his ship upwards, toward the safety of Earth's orbital defense grid, in a full retreat.

—

Water dragged against his soaked duster as William emerged from the ocean on the opposite side of the city. The force of the concussion of several missiles exploding on the surface of the water above him had nearly knocked him unconscious. As it was, his motorcycle was at the bottom of the bay and William was bleeding from his ears.

He crawled onto the sand unsteadily, his wet clothes hanging heavily around him, torn in several places. His three-barreled shotgun hanging loosely from its strap, he faced off with nearly fifty waiting UEDF soldiers who had seen him go in. The enemy commander was issuing orders that William could barely hear over the ringing of his ears.

The battered man grimaced as he tried to stand, falling back to his knees as the dizziness overwhelming his sense of balance. The familiar sound of the humming engines of a battle suit vessel grew louder by the second.

Looking up, he cocked his head curiously to the side as the dark samurai suit came into view. The soldiers saw it too and began running toward the buildings near the shore.

"I can feel the ships in orbit trying to lock onto us, we should go" Alex's voice said with a metallic echo, from the face of a dragon. "I can stop them, but it's taking a lot of concentration."

"Should I just climb on your back?" William stammered apprehensively, unsure if he had the strength to hold on.

In response, Alex motioned toward a small car that was mostly undamaged a short distance away. William walked to it and got inside, bracing himself.

The strong hands of *Skoll* lifted the car easily and the two began to fly low, over the water, to the north along the coastline. The shore flew by out the window as the leader of the revolution and his stepson made their escape.

CHAPTER 3

New Plan

AM I DREAMING?

It was a hazy thought as she opened her almond eyes. It had been so long since she saw the sweet, cherubic face of her youngest son. Connor's soft snoring took her mind back to simpler days. He wasn't the four-year-old child who she remembered, but other than being much taller, he looked almost the same.

Lying there, her mind replayed those years she had been away, leading the Independent Colonies, unable to return to Earth; the joy of being reunited with Alex and the frustration at losing him once more.

Her gaze moved from his face to his arm, where the smoldering remains of his OMBI blackened his skin. The memory of his last battle was fresh in her mind. The battle that left him comatose after he was deceived into fighting her and Alex, then betrayed by his commander.

She ran her fingers through Connor's hair before pulling herself weakly out of bed. Marlena Mercer, leader of the Independent Colonies, stretched her limbs as she stood. A stab of pain rippled through the side of her abdomen, reminding her of her own last battle. The operative's dead body still laid on the ground in her cargo hold where he fell, his face riddled with bullet holes.

She grimaced while inspecting where the operative's blade had struck her. The synthetic bonding gel had done its work, but it was going to need a lot more time before it was healed.

Putting on her slippers, she walked toward the flight deck, stopping, as she always did, to look at the pictures of her family on the wall of her cabin. She didn't linger today, forcing herself up the cold metal stairs into the flight deck of Tizona, Marlena's modified Anubis fighter.

She fell heavily into her chair, wincing as she checked her monitor. They had emerged from the slipstream on August 24th, 2121. Doing rough calculations in her head, Marlena realized it would be roughly another thirty-six hours until she could reliably communicate with Aeris VII. So she put on some music and made herself busy.

The time passed slowly in a haze of repairs and sleeping. She stayed out of the cargo hold, unable to face that macabre scene while it was so fresh in her mind. Each time she got near the door she found some excuse to not go through it. When Tizona was finally in range she immediately sent out her message.

"ICC command, this is Captain Mercer, over," she began reflexively, as she had every time she had emerged from a slipstream over the past six years.

"This is ICC command, welcome back, Captain," a man's voice said to her over the speaker one agonizing minute later.

"ICC command, ETA twelve hours. I will be landing on the hospital roof in Sapphire City. Please send word to Dr. Wagner and Engineer Evans from the 3rd fleet to meet me there. Also, pass word to the council that I need to speak with them immediately upon my return."

"Understood. Captain." The voice wavered. "Is everything okay?"

"Affirmative, Command, Captain Mercer out," she finished, not about to explain.

Marlena tossed down the headset and leaned back in her chair.

"Twelve hours," she muttered to herself.

She took a deep breath of stale, recycled air and swallowed a pain reliever before she walked back down to her bedroom. She had almost reached the door when a faint buzzing echoed through the speakers on her ship, then, a whisper.

"What?"

The buzzing grew louder as Marlena tensed up, glancing about anxiously. It got so loud that she had to cover her ears. The voices were unintelligible, parts of old songs and different people's voices played over a noise of a loud engine.

The cacophony ceased suddenly. Marlena took her hands from her ears and looked into her cabin at her sleeping son. Sweat dripped from his forehead and his breathing came out in labored gasps. She stepped into the room. A faint wisp of smoke wafted from his OMBI.

"That can't be good," Marlena said to herself, checking the boy's bracer. Though it wasn't hot to the touch, the smell of burnt wires permeated the room.

She moved slowly, carefully checking the rest of her ship in a medicated haze. Had she been more aware, she may have noticed the hatch she pulled Connor out of on Hati was now closed.

—

The ship was dark when she awoke from a bad dream. She had been running hard in the dream, but she couldn't quite remember if it was away or toward something. She wasn't sure how long she slept.

"We must be close by now," she said as she got out of bed.

Stumbling into the kitchen, she put on a pot of dark coffee. The floor lights illuminated the kitchen in a soft yellow glow.

It took her a moment to realize that the overhead lights hadn't come on like they were supposed to

A malfunction? The thought crossed her mind briefly. Her ship had taken some damage during the last fight, albeit light.

A blue light from the cargo bay caught her attention as she moved to the circuit panel. She peered through the doorway, freezing when she noticed the source of the light. Hati was sitting upright, the eyes on its wolfish face shining a furiously intense shade of blue.

Marlena gasped slightly, drawing the attention of the battle suit, which proceeded to growl softly.

"Where am I?" the ship asked in a low grumble, its mouth twisting into a snarl.

"In my cargo bay, on our way to the capitol of the independent colonies," Marlena answered firmly.

"Where is initiator?" Hati wheezed, sounding worried as its eyes settled on the corpse of the assassin that she had left on the floor nearby.

"Connor is asleep, upstairs," Marlena offered sympathetically. "He was hurt in battle. Do you know what happened to him?"

Hati's growl shook the ship as its face turned back toward the woman.

"Betrayed!" it roared, the word echoing in the cargo bay.

"I was betrayed by them too, years ago. But we can't focus on the past, we have to focus on what we can do right now. Can you help him?" Marlena pleaded.

"Must bring back friend," the vessel offered as the light in its eyes faded. "Omega."

After a moment of darkness, the lights of the ship re-activated normally.

The puzzled woman stood, staring at the battle suit for a long while, trying to sort out the meaning of the cryptic message. The thought was heavy on her mind when she made her way back up to the flight deck. Seeing Aeris VII coming into visual range even from the lower deck, she skipped the coffee pot and headed up to her flight controls.

Am I dreaming?

—

Tizona glided downward through the clear, purple sky, landing atop the tallest building in Sapphire City. The hospital was one of the newer buildings, built like a shiny tower that reflected the light of the sun. Marlena was greeted by a small group of doctors, including Doctor Franz Wagner, who specialized in biomechanics, and Earnest Evans, an Engineer from the 3rd fleet who had been studying the OMBI since the capture of black squadron during the battle of the Eagle Nebula.

"Captain Mercer! We're glad to have you back," Wagner offered as he walked forward.

His eyes went to her bloody shirt and he rushed forward ahead of a 311 AFMR.

"You're injured," He stated more than asked.

"I'm fine. I asked for you because Connor is onboard and he is hurt, bad," she said, turning away from the doctor.

Despite her claims to the contrary, Marlena was in a lot of pain and was beginning to wonder if her wound was infected. A medical hovering chair arrived for her and Doctor Wagner forced her to sit in it.

She tried to stand as the AFMR brought Connor out on a hovering gurney, but Wagner's firm hand kept her sitting.

"Let the doctors do their job; fussing over him won't help," he offered as they moved into the building.

Her scowl made Wagner recoil a bit.

"I'm sorry," he stammered.

The apology seemed to soften her scowl a bit. But she held on to it defiantly until they were well inside the building.

After a thorough examination, the AFMR insisted on re-opening her wound. Apparently there had been some minor internal bleeding that the bonding gel hadn't repaired. Despite her objections, she let the AFMR prepare her for surgery and, after an hour, was recovering in a room by herself.

Dr. Wagner and Engineer Evans entered her room a short time later to find Marlena tapping her foot impatiently. She looked at the two men expectantly as they sat beside her bed.

"We examined your son," Dr. Wagner began. "He is very strong to have survived what they did to him."

"What exactly did they do to him?" she whispered, not entirely over the effects of the anesthesia.

Engineer Evans took a deep breath before speaking, turning toward the window, unable to look the concerned woman in the eye as he spoke.

"As you probably remember, the first two inhibitor chips were designed to protect the students while they trained, slowing the bond and coming off to allow their OMBI manifestations to become more tangible. Since you left, we discovered that the 3rd chip was intended to stay, preventing the OMBI from being able to communicate back with the host. The 4th inhibitor, however, was the failsafe. It was designed to control the perceptions of the host and, if necessary, eliminate the wearer. It's likely that Connor somehow began overcoming the control function, so they detonated it."

"But it's on his arm, why is he comatose?" Marlena questioned, not fully understanding.

"Because the neuro-sync. The AI core in the bracer merges to the wearer's mind. The two, essentially, are designed to become one. We hypothesize that a strong mind at the right age, absent inhibitor chips and fully merged with an OMBI, would be unimaginably powerful. But all the reports that you forwarded to us from Major Sanders seemed to indicate that most minds couldn't handle it, not entirely anyway. In the last report we got of Connor's techno-psychological evaluation, it looked like he was forming the bonds subconsciously, bypassing the inhibitors," Evans finished, letting the weight of the information sink in.

The three were quiet after that for some time, digesting the information before Marlena spoke.

"My baby boy," she whispered to herself. Turning her eyes back to her friends, she asked, "What can we do for him? Can we take an OMBI from one of the kids of Black Squadron?"

"Theoretically," Evans began before Dr. Wagner cut him off with an upraised hand.

Dr. Wagner cleared his throat. "If we remove the OMBI from any of those kids, it's likely that they will die, or at best be comatose as well. It is possible that if we repaired Connor's OMBI AI chip, and installed it in another OMBI, the device would work normally. It's incredibly unlikely that we can use one of Black Squadron's bracers for that though. They are bonded with their host in ways we still don't fully understand. It would be like putting a dead man's brain in a living person's body and expecting that man to go about his life normally, except that we don't have anyone who understands how to perform that kind of a transplant."

Evans nodded his agreement as Dr. Wagner spoke.

"Our best chance would be to attach a new OMBI to Connor's other arm and see if it can repair the first," Evans offered uncertainly.

"Since we have observed OMBIs repairing themselves, it's the best theory we have come up with," Dr. Wagner finished.

Marlena sat staring at the wall, tapping her foot for nearly a minute before breaking the silence.

"It's a better plan than nothing, but you both should keep

working on other solutions. Until we can find a way to get into the OMBIcademy on Earth, to even get another OMBI, we have to find something else. Maybe Sanders can steal one, or ... dammit I don't know. There is an invasion fleet on the way here and we don't have the time..." she trailed off.

"You need to talk to the council," Evans began. "There may be another option. We received new information from Dr. Arminus on Dytopa II recently. It appears that the structure he discovered in the uninhabitable lands, near the Scorpio Sea, is another OMBIcademy ship, similar to the one on Earth."

"Have they been able to open it?" Marlena interrupted, the hope plain in her voice.

"No. If it's like the OMBIcademy on Earth, they will need an OMBI to open it." Evans shrugged.

Dr. Wagner hesitated. "If one of the soldiers from Black Squadron can be persuaded to help us, then it's possible that they could open the door. I think that the Omega Nebula is only about three thousand light years from here."

"Two thousand," Marlena corrected as she stood up. "I need to talk to the council, we have a lot to go over and not a lot of time. You two continue to work on what we need to make this work and make preparations to get those 4th inhibitors off the kids from Black Squadron. I'll see to it that you get authorization."

—

Setting up the video feed in the hospital was easy enough, although getting the council together for an emergency session took longer than Marlena would have liked. She had been getting regular updates on Connor's condition as she waited, letting the bonding gels in her side settle and harden into flesh.

It was evening when the council finally assembled. Commanders Watson and Clarke were the last to join, having been busy overseeing the repairs of the fleet from the attack on Aeris. They had lost two hundred twenty-two crew members and two frigates in the battle. It would have been far worse had Alex not intervened in Skoll, having almost singlehandedly ended the battle in a matter of minutes. Finding new assignments for the surviving crew members hadn't been difficult, but training them for new positions was taking time. Both commanders were proactive men and took a personal interest in the soldiers under their command.

Commander Watson began the video call as soon as all five Independent Colony leaders had assembled.

"I apologize for the delay. How are your injuries, Captain? How is your son?" The edge of concern marked his questions with sincere worry.

"I'm okay. Connor was betrayed by his commander during a battle with Alex and me. He's in a coma, but alive." She wrestled the despair out of her voice as she continued, "They knew we were coming. Alex stayed to fight and I haven't heard from him since. As you're all probably already aware, the operative that had been spying on us here had stowed away on Tizona and tried to assassinate me during the fighting."

Representative Gellar gasped on the screen.

"We haven't heard from Alex but he has the frequency of your communication relay. When you're feeling well enough you should try to make contact and check with your contacts on Earth to see if you can get any information on his whereabouts," Watson suggested.

"That was my plan, Commander. But I wanted to contact the council first and let you know that our mission to intercept the escaping enemy frigates failed. There is likely an invasion force in slipstream, headed our way as we speak," Marlena warned.

The weight of the comment settled on the council for several seconds before Representative Gellar broke the silence.

"I don't mean to get off such an important subject," she began slowly, "but how did you manage to kill an operative, and remain relatively unscathed?"

All of the members of the council waited quietly for the answer. Despite the urgency of the situation, they were all curious. The skills of the operatives were almost mythical.

"My sons were in danger. I knew that if I lost, they would die, so I did what I had to," she answered simply, letting the comment sink in before adding, "And I wouldn't say that I got away unscathed."

When no one spoke, Marlena changed the subject back to the situation at hand.

"We need to have the fleets on standby to defend Aeris, assuming that is the target of the invasion force; it seems likely though. Our orbital defenses aren't nearly complete and even with the full strength of our fleets, we are severely outgunned," she finished cryptically.

Captain Velez spoke for the first time since the communication began.

"Should we make plans to evacuate Aeris?" he asked plainly.

"I don't think so," Marlena said. "They need our civilian population to continue to produce resources for the UEDF to remain in power on Earth. Besides, without Aeris to protect all the colonies, where would everyone go?"

"You're probably right," Velez conceded.

"What about surrender?" Representative Gellar asked before adding, "If we were so heavily outgunned, I would want to spare as many lives as possible."

"Let's not surrender before we know the strength of the enemy force," Commander Watson barked quickly. "Also, there is no guarantee that our surrender would even be accepted. Likely, General Harruhama thinks of all us as traitors to be executed."

"We also need to consider the rebellion on Earth. The last

report I got said that in a lot of areas the rebels were winning. Two of the Earth Military Council members are dead already and there is always the potential of sympathizers in the enemy ranks. Remember, there were no independent fleets six years ago," Commander Clarke explained in his baritone voice.

Being of the three commanders who had been ordered to retake the colonies, he knew well how dissatisfied the military was of the EMC's leadership. Of the other two commanders who were sent to the hourglass nebula to retake Aeris, one was dead and the other was Commander Watson.

"Besides," Clarke continued, "once our enemies see Tizona and know that Phoenix is alive, they won't be able to help but question the legitimacy of the EMC."

"Actually, Commander Clarke, I may not be here for the fight," Marlena interjected. "I am planning on taking Connor to the Omega Nebula. There is a chance that I could be able to revive him there."

"I see." Clarke paused. "I can only imagine how you feel about your son, but this could be the turning point, our freedom or our extinction. Can it wait?"

It was a difficult question for Clarke to ask. He knew well the sacrifices that Marlena had already made for the Independent Colonies but, as a Council Member, he still had to ask it.

Marlena was quiet for a long while, weighing the responsibility to the people she led against the love she had for her child. In the end it wasn't really a decision.

"I am going to the Omega Nebula as soon as I can. I need to contact Earth and I need the council's permission to release as many of the prisoners from Black Squadron as will volunteer to go with me when we remove their 4th inhibitor chips. If the mission is successful, I can be back in time to join the fight," She decided.

She stated it as a fact, not leaving room in her tone for

debate. Having recognized her as their leader for six years, everyone on the council knew the futility of arguing with the fiery woman once she had made up her mind.

—

A short time after the transmission ended, Marlena Mercer walked slowly down the white hospital halls toward the room her youngest son lay asleep in. She watched him from the door for a few moments, as she had many times before the EMC had separated them, then she walked over to him and kissed his forehead.

"I hate to go, my sweet baby boy," she whispered, "but I have to check on Alex. I'll be back soon and we will go get you all fixed up, I promise."

With a heavy heart she made her way to the roof and boarded her Anubis fighter.

The flight from Sapphire City through the Grimnir Mountains to where she had built the communications array only took thirty minutes, but on that particular day it seemed to take forever to Marlena, whose thoughts were consumed by the safety of her sons.

She was still weak from the surgery, but the doctors who treated her had given her some pain medication to get by, until her wounds were fully healed. They had recommended a week of bed rest but, with the clock ticking on an invasion and the galaxy at war, she just didn't have the time.

The lush green hills rolled by unnoticed while she sat quietly in her chair, reading as much as could about the situation on Earth and the information about the other OMBIcademy vessel.

She felt her ship descend and, as Tizona set down on the grassy hill, she grabbed her data pad and walked to the array through the cargo bay, which was still stained with blood. She eyed Hati dubiously, still trying to sort out whether or not the conversation she had with the machine about her son was a dream. She shuddered as she walked by.

Her dark hair danced in the wind as she crossed the hill. She casually tied it back to keep it from becoming a distraction. Sitting down against the familiar tree and taking a deep breath, she prepared herself for the two people she had to contact. She was so nervous about whether or not Alex was safe, that she let fear make her procrastinate.

"Sanders here," the familiar voice groaned.

Her call had clearly awoken the man. The image was dark on the screen, except for the tired face of the aging soldier, illuminated softly by the light of the datapad he held.

"Sorry to wake you, Major, but we received word that there may be an impending attack against the Independent Colonies. Can you confirm this?" she questioned, knowing the distortion field of the array would keep the transmission from being traced on Earth.

"Harruhama ordered the invasion nearly three weeks ago. It's not a small force; he sent the entire 2nd, 6th, 7th, and 8th fleets against you," Sanders explained, the fatigue evident in his tone.

Marlena did the math in her head, seventy-six total frigates, fifteen Anubis squadrons. Unless any of those fleets had ships down for maintenance, against her thirty-one frigates, two of which were being repaired, and five operating Anubis Squadrons, they were outnumbered more than 2:1. Worse for the Independent Colonies, some of their frigates hadn't completed the slipstreams back from their tours on other colonies.

"I see," she said while tapping her teeth with her finger. "Is there any reason to suspect that these fleets are traveling faster than a normal slipstream?"

"No, as far as I know the experimental battle suit vessels, Hati and Skoll, are the only ones that can accelerate a slipstream and I don't think either of them is with the invasion force," Sanders explained.

"Thank you, Major," Marlena said as she always had just before terminating the transmission.

"Wait," Sanders blurted. "There's something else."

"What is it?"

"Two things really. First, Connor was taken from the OMBIcademy for specialized training. I don't know where he is now."

"Yes I know, what's the other?"

"William Mercer is alive. He is leading the rebellion on Earth. At least, he was three months ago."

"What?" she asked breathlessly, feeling the tears well up in her eyes.

"William Mercer is the Dragoon," Sanders stated simply.

"Oh my God…" She trailed off, stunned by the news that her husband, whom she had thought dead for the last six months, was alive and fighting the other side of the same war.

"Thank you, Edmond," she said using his first name for the second time in five years.

She let the transmission end with that, unable to continue.

She sobbed on the mountaintop. Overwhelmed, she let the chaos of her emotions out. Tears rolled down cheeks, falling onto her shirt. The thought of William fighting and leading a rebellion in her memory gave her strength. Despite all that there was still to do, Marlena smiled, wiping the tears on her sleeve. She took several deep breaths to steady herself and, finding her resolve, began the next transmission she had come to make.

—

The charred remains lay in tatters as Alex examined what had been his childhood home in Healdsburg, California. He hadn't been there in nearly six years and had forgotten how much the smell of the Russian River Valley felt like home. He and William had escaped the ruins of San Francisco and had been camping out on the remains of the Mercer Estate.

A pile of burnt wood and metal beams sat where the house used to be, littering the yard and where the pool was. None of the statues had survived the blast either, but the garage and workshop still stood, although they were in poor shape. The entire structure leaned heavily upon an old oak tree.

Skoll was kneeling in the garage, a hammock swaying between its strong arms. William had been asleep on it since before Alex had left on a supply run in town. The rebellion hadn't quite taken hold in Healdsburg, as there weren't many UEDF facilities in the area, which made supply runs as simple as heading to the local grocery store. Food had become dangerously scare, but in the fertile valley, many goods were still available.

His hands were beginning to turn black with soot as he half-heartedly picked through the rubble, looking for anything that might have survived. He didn't like being away from the fighting but, glancing back at the garage, he knew that his stepfather had needed him. The man had died for the revolution that he started. Although he lacked the increased strength and endurance that Alex had with his OMBI, the strange mechanized battle suit that William wore seemed to keep him going, long after fatigue should have stopped him.

Alex was covered in soot when his OMBI lit up with a transmission from Aeris VII's communication array. The worry for his mother melted away even before he answered.

"Hi, Mom," Alex chirped with a boyish smile as the holographic image of his mother appeared from his OMBI.

"Thank God you're okay, Alex! Why didn't you come back with us to Aeris? Where are you?" Marlena's relief and worry came through clearly in her frantic voice.

Alex panned the shot around so his mom could see.

"I'm home, Mom. At least, where it used to be. I got hit before I could slipstream back to you and ended up too close to Earth. They shot me down, if you can believe it," Alex chuckled.

"I believe it! The orbital defense grid is nasty around Earth. Are you okay? Did your ship survive?" she questioned sympathetically.

"Yeah, I hate that defense grid. I'm fine. My ship was damaged and I had to abandon it for a few days while the UEDF tried to corner me, but it repaired itself and I got it back. You'll never guess who saved me from the UEDF though," Alex teased excitedly.

She was silent for a moment. It was obvious that she knew already, but almost as if she was afraid to say his name.

"William?" she whispered.

"How did you know?" Alex chuckled delightedly.

"Is he with you now?" she asked with a breathless hint of excitement in her voice.

In response Alex walked to the hammock where William was sleeping, his wide-brimmed cowboy hat resting over his eyes.

The hologram of Marlena was smiling as she saw the man for the first time in six years.

Awakened by Alex's approach, William lifted the hat from his eyes, letting his jaw drop as he looked at the face of his wife, the woman he had loved since the minute he met her.

The two quietly stared at each other for a long minute.

"You got older, Azucar," Marlena said, looking at the man's tired eyes.

"Yeah, losing your family and dying will do that to you," he replied whimsically. "You haven't changed a bit, still as beautiful as the day we met."

Tears were forming in his eyes as she smiled at him, blushing. He'd always had a way of melting her with his words. The rebellion and time apart felt distant as the moments passed. Neither of them seemed to know how to say what they were thinking.

Finally Alex broke the silence. "Is Connor okay, Mom? What happened? I lost your communications before you slipped out."

"I was attacked by a damn operative who had stowed away on Tizona, Alex. I'm pretty sure it was the same one who attacked you that night of the battle in Sapphire City. He stabbed me, but I'm okay," she finished quickly, padding the air to calm them.

"Connor's 4th inhibitor was detonated by whoever was leading that attack against us. He's in a coma," she continued somberly. Both Alex and William grimaced at the news.

"It was Harruhama, Mom," he growled. "That frigate was the Nostus, it's the flagship of the 1st fleet."

William's fists clenched with rage, and through gritted teeth he muttered, "I almost had him. The day he took Connor from the OMBIcademy he personally arrived to take him, in order to get him to fight against you both. I'll kill him."

Alex held no doubts at William's claim, the severity of his voice causing Marlena to look at him with concern.

"We have a plan for how to help Connor, but we have to go the Omega Nebula colony. The ship that Dr. Arminus found is another OMBIcademy vessel and we are hoping to find a new OMBI for Connor. The idea is that, the way that they heal will repair his mind and his old OMBI," she explained, "What do you think, Alex?"

Alex was nodding as she finished. "That sounds like it could work; in fact, I can't even think of any other way to help him. That structure on Dytopa II was another OMBIcademy? How are you going to unlock it? Do you need me to slipstream there?"

"No, stay with William and help the rebels on Earth for now. There are four fleets heading toward Aeris VII as we speak and the best way to protect the Independent Colonies now is to end the war before they get here. They are travelling through a normal slipstream. They left three weeks ago so we have about seven more weeks before they arrive. I'm not far from Dytopa II and will go with Connor. I'm going to recruit some of the Black Squadron prisoners to help me open it."

Alex's shook his head and pursed his lips at that.

"You will need to remove their 4th inhibitors before asking them and even then, there are no guarantees. They are all very dangerous with their OMBI so be careful with them. They are good soldiers but still under UEDF influence. Knock them out, strap them down, remove the inhibitor, and tell them who you are. Your best bet is with Pip Michaels and Mimelia Pierce, they go by Anataur and Artemis. They are like, best friends, and of the survivors you have there, those two are probably the strongest. Also, Mimelia has always admired you and if she recognizes you, will probably volunteer."

"Thanks, Alex, that's going to help a lot!" Marlena said, furiously taking notes on her datapad.

William and Marlena both smiled at Alex, making him look away, flustered.

"Oh, by the way," William chimed in, "if you can stomach wearing a dead man's clothes, that operative you defeated might have been wearing some pretty serious battle armor. I killed one and took his a couple months ago. It has kept me alive through a lot of stuff that should have killed me. I can't even tell you what it's made out of. I think it's alien tech."

"I'll see if it fits," Marlena remarked dryly. "Thank you, William. Keep my baby safe. I have to get going. It's a long way to Dytopa II."

"It was good to hear your voice, Marlena. I've missed you, every day." William smiled.

"I missed you too, William. I love you," she said, turning back to Alex. "I love you, Alex."

"I love you," William said, unable to stop the tears.

"Love you, Mom," Alex finished as the image of Marlena faded.

William smiled at Alex, who was smiling back.

"Connor is going to be okay, it's a good plan," Alex offered, scrolling through his OMBI menus.

"I know he will. What are you doing?" William asked.

"Well, we need to stop a war and topple a government. I'm trying to find out where we can find Harruhama."

"We can always interrogate his officers. Where has the rebellion made the most progress that we can get to reasonably quickly?" William asked thoughtfully.

"Good idea. It looks like some areas of the Midwest have completely brought down the UEDF troops. Texas, Iowa, near Des Moines, New York, Seattle ... you pick."

"Nice to see that the leaders I left behind did a good job. Let's get in the air and start heading east. Make contact with the Free Men leaders in those areas and try to figure out who has the best selection of prisoners," William finished.

"What about your nap?" Alex quipped as he began to take down the hammock and load his gear.

William smiled back at his stepson, smirking at the joke.

"I couldn't sleep even if I wanted to."

CHAPTER 4

Unexpected Allies

S HE WAS ALREADY TAPPING ON HER DATAPAD BY THE TIME Tizona lifted off the ground. Marlena was sending instructions to Engineer Evans to remove the inhibitor chips from Pip and Mimelia as Alex had suggested. That message sent, she began firing off messages to the council about the status of the invasion fleet's estimated date of arrival in the Hourglass Nebula.

Tizona's autopilot taking her back to Sapphire City, she went into the kitchen and poured a cup of coffee. Marlena smiled thinking of her conversation with Alex and William. William! She felt butterflies in a way she hadn't felt in years.

As she sipped her coffee, she walked into her room to look at the pictures she had on her wall again. Her eyes moved from William to Alex and then settled on a picture of Connor. She sighed deeply, the smile fading from her face. Not sure what to expect from Dytopa II, the information she had on the "beast storms" in the area around where the OMBIcademy ship caused a chill to roll up her spine. She decided then to take William's advice about the operative's armor.

—

Under the purple sunrise, a chilling breezed rolled off the Grimnir

Mountains, over the waters off Lake Amsvartnir, and across the valley just north of Sapphire City, where the remains of an old battle frigate rested at the base of a small, wooded hill. The hulking mass had once been the flagship of the 4th fleet, but like all the other ships of the 4th, it was now decommissioned and re-purposed for colony life.

It had been used for scrap-metal and electronics, until the need for a prison arose after the battle of the Eagle Nebula. It now stood as the heavily guarded home for the remains of the OMBI-soldiers from Black Squadron, nineteen of the most dangerous teenagers in the galaxy.

Evans's transport rolled to a stop in front of the loading bay as the engineer of the 3rd fleet finished reading the instructions that Marlena had sent him. He departed with a sigh and walked a familiar path through the rusted hallways; murmured anti-Gortha slurs followed him as he passed each cell.

Many of the cells were in bad shape, punctured and crumbling from where the soldiers had manifested weapons and attempted escape. Heavy physical bars blocked the doorways, replacing the electronic locks that had been overridden through an OMBI.

Evans removed the datapad from his labcoat pocket and pressed his spectacles against his face with a quivering hand. He began reading the descriptions of the two soldiers who he had come to collect.

He found Mimelia Pierce easily enough, as she was one of the only two surviving girls from Black Squadron. Her pale, short hair shimmered in the dim overhead lighting while she stalked about her cell. Many punctures littered the walls from where she had tried to break free.

Reading the dossier, Evans' eyes grew wide: *They called her Artemis as she excels with the bow and has even found ways of adapting her OMBI manifestations to make the weapon a versatile tool, bringing grappling hook ladders, explosives, remote sentries and homing rockets into battle. Although she avoids conventional weaponry unless absolutely necessary, Artemis is considered an extreme threat.*

Evans looked from the datapad through the porthole window to see fierce brown eyes staring back at him. It happened instantly; before he could react to the movement, Artemis had manifested her black bow and fired off two quick arrows straight into the reinforced glass. The screeching of metal on glass caused Evans to fall back against the wall behind him.

"Well, I never…" Evans stammered, finding his feet.

A nearby guard snorted a laugh, which earned a glower from Evans.

"Sedate her and radio a shuttle for transport," Evans barked, sending the guard off.

The guard was still grinning when he moved down the hall to the control room.

Making notes, Evans moved down the hall until he found the room of Pip Michaels. The door was unmistakable, as the six-inch steel bulged dangerously into the hallway in several spots. A feral growl emerged from the cell before Evans got to the porthole, causing him to freeze and look to his dossier.

They called him Anataur and his weapon of choice is the battle hammer. Within minutes of his confinement, he had almost broken down his cell door until he had been neutralized by sedative gas. We have had to sedate him each time he has manifested a weapon from then on. The dosage is at near lethal levels, as Anataur seems to be developing an immunity. Consider his threat level: nightmare.

Evans re-read the last sentence before managing an unsteady breath. His knees shook as he peered into the cell. Sweat poured from the boy's face and body as he grunted out push-ups in a steady cadence. Without any precursor, the shirtless mountain of a boy hopped to his feet and narrowed his blue eyes at Evans.

The boy looked to his OMBI and back at the door with a calculated gaze before turning away in a huff.

Evans turned away from the cell and began walking toward the command center. Anataur's frustrated roar followed him, causing Evans to run the rest of the way.

When Evans arrived at the command center, Artemis was already being taken to the transport, sleeping soundly upon a hovering gurney.

"Sedate Anataur and load him up next," Evans offered to the guards in the control room.

Two nervous guards made their way down to the cell with the bulging door. They waited nearly two minutes before the heard the thump of the boy falling to the ground. When the gas had cleared, they struggled to lift him, picking up his upper body first, then swinging his legs onto the gurney.

"Hey." Anataur grinned, his eyes popping open.

The guard immediately reached for the sedative syringe but Anataur caught his hand, twisting it back violently.

"Not so fast!" the boy barked, hopping onto unsteady feet.

Anataur stumbled and fell against the bed on the opposite side of the room, shaking his head.

The second guard ran forward, slamming into his side, bouncing off the stout boy.

Anataur set his feet, swaying about with raised fists, forcing the two guards back. A swift right hook caught one of the guards on the temple, knocking him to the ground. As the second guard came around, Anataur grabbed his fist and forced his arm behind his back. The boy quickly locked the older guard into a sleeper hold and squeezed until the man fell unconscious.

"Dang weak, Gortha, how did they even capture us?" He yawned, blinking several times.

Anataur stumbled into the hallway, bouncing off another cell door, and staggered. He took a few running steps and bounced off another. Growling, he shut his eyes and charged forward, bursting through the command center door.

A sledge hammer twice the size of Anataur began to manifest in his hands before it crumbled away. Six armed soldiers tackled him and forced him to the ground as the base commander ran to a set of lockers and produced a long rifle.

"No, don't shoot him!" Evans pleaded.

"Relax, it's a tranquilizer," the commander said calmly as he lined up his shot.

The dart plunged into the boy's neck, followed by a second. His inhuman strength seemed to diminish until he collapsed in a heap. The guards gathered themselves, staring wide-eyed at the dangerous OMBI-soldier, who had begun snoring loudly.

They strapped him tightly down to the gurney and escorted Evans to the shuttle bay, where his transport awaited.

"Whatever you have planned," the base commander offered, looking at Evans, "I'd do it quick."

Looking back at the Black Squadron soldiers, Evans only bobbed his head in agreement.

—

Marlena was brushing the hair off the face of her son while he laid unconscious in his hospital room when the prison transport arrived. She had returned to Sapphire City ahead of Evans and was getting impatient.

"Took you long enough," she chided when Evans entered the room.

"There was a complication. Are you sure about this? These two are very dangerous," he warned.

"We need them. I will be in the room with you when you remove their inhibitors," she said, rising to her feet.

"I'm sure I can get soldiers for that," Evans began.

"No, I want to see what my sons have gone through. Besides, seeing inside the OMBI might help when I go to Dytopa," she explained.

Evans nodded at her reasoning and bit back a comment. He knew better than to argue with her.

The operating theater was down one floor and by the time Evans and Marlena arrived the two OMBI soldiers were waiting for them.

An AFMR waited beside the operating table, next to Artemis.

"Is this a complicated procedure?" Marlena asked, looking at the machine.

"No, according to Captain Pereira, it's pretty simple," Evans spoke up, before the AFMR could answer.

"Let me," she said, taking the drill from the AFMR's arm.

The drill whistled as she unfastened the small bolts. She gently pulled the face-plate off with her fingers and opened the case where the inhibitors were housed. Two slots were empty. Marlena examined the other two, skipping the 3rd chip and gripping the 4th with pliers.

Beads of sweat formed upon Artemis' brow as Marlena began to pull. The younger girl's eyelids began to flutter and her breath came in short gasps. Marlena and Engineer Evans exchanged glances, and with one quick tug Marlena pulled the chip out. The removal of the chip caused the sweating to decrease slightly, and as Marlena re-attached the faceplate the girl began to visibly relax. As the last screw went in, she appeared to be back in a peaceful slumber as if nothing had happened.

Moving to the other patient, Engineer Evans took the lead. His drill whirled as the faceplate of the OMBI was removed. Using the pliers, he gripped and pulled at the 4th inhibitor.

Anataur's bloodshot eyes popped open, followed by a scream of rage.

"What are you doing to me?" he cried.

Fighting against the restraints, Anataur had his left arm nearly free when Marlena grabbed it with both hands and threw her weight against it. She felt herself lift off the ground as the straps began to fail.

"Calm down, Michaels!" she screamed, which only fueled the tirade as the boy began to kick against his leg bindings, sweat pouring from his forehead and body.

"I can't get the cover back on!" Evans cried, fighting to get his drill into place.

In the struggle, Marlena missed the tearing of straps behind her and fell back in shock as a lithe form leapt on top of Anataur.

Artemis pinned Anataur down using the strength of her OMBI-infused arms.

"Get that back on," she ordered Engineer Evans, nodding toward Anataur's OMBI.

"Shh," she soothed, looking into Anataur's eyes. "It's okay, big guy."

"What are they doing to me?" Anataur sputtered, looking back at her.

"It's okay, Pip. We are going to be okay," she cooed.

Anataur's shoulders relaxed and he stopped struggling as the whistle of the drill stopped. The boy looked around the room, blinking several times.

"Where are the Gortha, Mimi?" Pip asked.

"I don't think there ever were any. This woman," she smiled, "is the Phoenix."

—

An hour later the pair were calm and were talking at a table in the hospital cafeteria. Anataur had a mouthful of spiced chicken when Marlena and Evans approached them.

"What's going on, where are we even?" Anataur asked bluntly, smiling up at Marlena.

Every soldier in the UEDF knew the story of the Phoenix and her death at the hands of the Gortha in the Incident of 2115. The Phoenix, as a martyr, had been an icon of the recruiting effort of the military ever since.

She looked back and forth between them and smiled.

"I am Captain Marlena Mercer, the Phoenix," she began, introducing herself. "I wasn't killed in 2115 as the reports said. I was betrayed by the UEDF, which resulted in the creation of the Independent Colonies. Your 4th inhibitor chips were designed to trick you into thinking we were your enemy. You are in the hospital on Aeris VII, capitol of the Independent Colonies."

Artemis was nodding along thoughtfully while Anataur's face scrunched up in confusion.

"What does she mean?" Anataur whispered.

"She means we were being lied to and she was attacked by the UEDF, a few times I think," Artemis explained.

Looking back at Marlena, she continued, "That is why Mephisto turned on us in the Eagle Nebula. I had been wondering about that, it didn't make sense that the Gortha could control his mind but didn't bother with any of the rest of us."

"You're pretty sharp," Marlena complimented while nodding along with the younger girl's assessment. "That is pretty much it. Right now Alex is on Earth leading a rebellion against the UEDF, which has sent four fleets against us. Moreover, Alex's brother, Connor, had his 4th inhibitor detonated and is laying in a coma upstairs."

She let the weight of her statement settle on the two teenagers. Artemis nodded thoughtfully; Anataur took another bite of chicken.

"The last time I talked to him, Alex suggested that I remove the inhibitors from you both. He said that you two were the best suited to be able to help me revive my son."

Anataur pushed his plate away and looked back at her. Neither of them missed the desperation in her voice.

"What can we do? We're not doctors or engineers..." Anataur offered.

"I'm going to take Connor to Dytopa II, in the Omega Nebula where there is another OMBIcademy. The first one, where you trained, is actually the ruins of an alien ship, and we have reason to believe that this other one might have the technology necessary to help him. But we don't have a lot of time."

"You need someone to open the doors," Artemis nodded. "If it is the same system we can probably help get you in, although there were a lot of doors in the OMBIcademy on Earth that neither of us could open. It's been a while since either of us has been there, but we're a lot stronger now."

"Yes, but that's not all. Dytopa II's lowlands suffer from massive electric storms, which are followed by the swarms of beasts that live there. It could be very dangerous and during the storms there is no way we can fly in, we have to go by land. I won't force you to go with me but I honestly don't have any other options. Will you come with me and help me save my son?" Marlena pleaded.

"I am not afraid of any beasts or storms," Anataur touted, "and if Mephisto recommended me personally, then I have to go."

"Thank you," Marlena said, smiling before turning her head to Artemis.

"You can count me in too," she said without hesitating. "In fact, it has always been my dream to serve beside the Phoenix."

—

Marlena dressed in the mechanized battle armor of an operative. She forced away the memory of the man who had worn it while she moved through some basic combat motions. Unearthly strength flowed into her limbs and she somehow felt more agile.

"This will do," she muttered.

She emerged into the hallway outside the locker room to find Anataur and Artemis waiting for her. With a nod, she led the two soldiers from Black Squadron toward the landing pad, where Tizona awaited.

Artemis ran ahead and inspected the ship, her mouth agape.

"I can't believe this is Tizona? Is she really faster than any ship in the fleet?" she sputtered.

Anataur smiled at Marlena and shrugged. "She's been a fan-girl of yours forever. Sorry about this."

Despite the situation, Marlena just smiled.

Engineer Evans led a hovering capsule onto the landing pad, stealing the mirth of the moment. Inside, Connor's comatose body lay perfectly still.

They watched as he loaded it into the cargo bay on Tizona.

"Good luck, Captain Mercer," he offered as he walked back onto the landing pad.

"Thank you for all your help," she replied, with a brief hug.

Anataur and Artemis both warily eyed the imposing form of Hati as they entered Tizona's cargo bay. Neither of them could forget what a similar-looking ship had done to Black Squadron when Alex had turned on them.

The battle suit seemed to crouch protectively over Connor's tube.

They proceeded through the ship quickly, walking to the flight deck. Anataur plopped into the gunner seat while Artemis sat in the navigator's chair, though both stations were redundant on Tizona since Marlena had modified it to operate all three stations from the helm.

"Can I fly?" Artemis asked hopefully.

Marlena shook her head, as she fired up the engines.

"You don't know until you try." Artemis shrugged at Anataur.

The ship lifted up into the purple sky of Aeris VII, setting a path between the two dim moons before breaking out of the atmosphere. It would take nearly twenty days to get to the Omega Nebula under a normal slipstream and Marlena didn't waste any time.

—

Vertigo walked anxiously through the cold halls of the Nostus. It had only been a few days since his defeat in San Francisco and the repairs to Fenris were taking longer than he had hoped. When he had broken through the atmosphere, he'd received orders from General Harruhama himself to dock with the UEDF flagship.

The days went by quietly, largely due to the 1st fleet rallying its forces between Mars and Earth defensively. With the absence of the other fleets, Earth was more vulnerable than it had been in a long time.

It was early in the morning when Vertigo had been summoned by Harruhama to meet in a remote observation lounge. A plainly dressed guard eyed him as he approached. The two shared a quiet nod as the boy entered the room.

The domed ceiling offered an amazing view of the endless sea of stars and Vertigo almost missed the older Japanese man waving him over to the other side of the long room.

Harruhama held himself with an imposing severity as he turned away from his stargazing.

"Do you know why I fought so hard to put the EMC in charge of the UEDF?" the aging general asked, facing away from the boy.

"In order to be better prepared for the Gortha threat to Earth and the colonies," Austin recited. The information was common knowledge and mentioned nearly every time any of the Earth Military Council were on a holotube report.

The old man coughed a bit as he chuckled.

"There is a lot you don't know. The truth goes far deeper than any media tagline. As I get older and look back at the campaign I started as a very young man, I begin to wonder if any of it was worth it," Harruhama explained, in a rare moment of nostalgia.

"Of course it is, sir. The Gortha have agents that I have fought, they even made my commander turn against us. They are a cunning adversary."

"They are indeed." Harruhama nodded, turning back toward the window of the observation lounge.

Far below the UEDF Nostus, Earth spun quietly in the darkness of space. "It looks so peaceful from here. Did you know that I didn't start my military career until I was in my late twenties? I was an electronic security specialist, back when the world still had internet security concerns. I was good too. I had even developed a way to track the wireless frequencies that were accessing all the global systems. The framework I developed is still used today to track datapad access and even in your bracer."

Vertigo listened quietly, his mind trying to connect this information with his role in the UEDF.

"This is something I have never told anybody but, right before I joined the military, I discovered a signal coming from the bottom of the Pacific Ocean, reaching out into every security system on Earth."

"What was it?" Vertigo asked, growing curious.

"That question has been plaguing me for over thirty-five years, young man. We can't unmake our choices but, I will tell you this, my..." the general coughed before continuing, "our future depends on defeating the rebels and getting back our colonies."

The boy nodded carefully.

"I won't let you down again, sir," he said after a moment.

"See that you don't, Hughes. To help you, we have repaired your Fenris and added some additional tech," Harruhama explained. "Moreover, you will be working with another operative to ensure that you do not fail again."

Out of the corner of his eye, Vertigo finally noticed the man standing next to him, the guard from the corridor.

"This is Operative 2. He will be joining you in the hunt for the rebel leaders and the Gortha ship you were chasing," Harruhama said, introducing the plain-looking man.

The boy eyed the operative carefully, wondering how, even with his senses enhanced by his OMBI, the man had managed to sidle up next to him unnoticed.

"Okay, I'm ready," Vertigo said, after a moment.

"Then you are dismissed. Do not fail me again," the old general warned, leaving Vertigo to follow the operative out of the room.

—

The operative led the way to the hanger, walking casually, keeping his back to Vertigo.

"I'm Vertigo," the boy said, introducing himself.

The other man stopped in the hall and without turning simply said, "I am Operative Two."

The awkward introductions out of the way, the two continued down to the hanger, where the rattle of machinery and repairs echoed. The hum of the Nostus engines was louder in the fighter bays and Vertigo accepted the ear plugs that a nearby mechanic offered him. They walked to where Fenris was waiting alongside a strange ship that he thought was a huge pile of fuel hoses at first.

The thing looked like a coiled snake, pale in color except

for the head, which was painted red. It wasn't tall in its coiled form, only about half the height of Fenris' thirty feet, but the coils seemed to go on and on so that he couldn't tell how large it would be when fully extended. Upon closer inspection, he could see that the scales of the snake were made up of even smaller scales that interlocked.

"What is it called?" Vertigo all but yelled to the grinning operative.

"*Jörmungandr*," the operative answered, looking back. "The Midgard Serpent."

Vertigo nodded at the fitting name before walking to where Fenris waited quietly. He couldn't tell what additions had been made to his ship but the repairs seemed complete. He climbed up into the cockpit and slid his arms and legs into place, feeling the familiar strength of his ship as it began to power up.

～

Small towns passed by the window as Skoll carried the small car low over abandoned highways in the Midwest.

"Where is everybody?" Alex asked through his OMBI.

"Global shipping has frozen. There probably isn't much fuel anywhere anymore," William speculated through his datapad.

The two had communicated in this way throughout the flight, Alex letting Skoll soar while William sat comfortably in the passenger seat of the car.

"That makes sense. By the way, did you catch that last report on the global net?"

"Which one? I read that most of the UEDF forces have been removed from Europe and Asia, except in a few major cities. Your OMBI probably fed you more than I could read on my datapad though." William shrugged.

"Yeah, that one. It sounded like most of the regional troops and police joined up with the free men and started rallying to ration food," Alex confirmed.

"I hope Harruhama doesn't resort to orbital bombing in those areas," William mused aloud.

Alex was quiet. He hadn't seen the bombing in New York, but William had told him all about it.

Outside of Des Moines, Alex landed in a park that had been unmolested by the war, though the grass was brown and dead throughout most of it. Leaving Skoll under a small grove of trees, Alex and William drove the car toward town.

They had just reached the city limits when they hit the free men road block.

"You're the Dragoon, aren't you?" the surprised rebel asked as William stopped the car.

"Yeah, that's right." William grinned.

"Drive on through, our command center is in the center of town. Commander Weiss will want to talk to you!"

Thanking the rebel, William followed the instructions and drove to the center of town, where they found the free man headquarters at city hall.

Alex and William were led into a small office and were talking when the door opened. Several armed men walked in led by a sandy-haired man in his early twenties.

"It's really you," the commander said after a moment, extending his hand.

William shook the man's hand, seeing the spark of recognition.

"Have we met?" William asked, raising an eyebrow.

"Not exactly. I was a guard, manning a tower at the

Clarion Detention Facility when you attacked. I was the only one that survived," Weiss explained, locking eyes with William.

"I'm not sure what to say," William said, shifting uncomfortably.

"It was a hard time for me. You had wiped out my unit and hearing your speech to the prisoners there, I didn't know what to do. I was so angry at them for not following you. I went AWOL and wandered for a bit. I was in a bar watching Councilman Stahl's presentation about you when I saw the video about the betrayal of the Phoenix and I snapped. I rallied anyone I could and we pushed the UEDF troops out of Iowa," Weiss finished, nodding to his fellow free men.

"Well, I'm glad my words got through to somebody there. To be totally honest, I was feeling a bit conflicted after Clarion too. Those prisoners were supposed to be the revolutionaries but, in the end, they were the ones who were all talk and the true free men were quietly all around us just needing a spark," William offered respectfully.

"Thank you for all of it, Dragoon." Weiss nodded.

"Thank you, Commander Weiss." William nodded back.

Reluctant to interrupt the moment, Alex cleared his throat, drawing the attention of the men in the room.

"We are here because we were hoping to get some information on the whereabouts of General Harruhama and the other leaders of the UEDF. You had been doing so well here we thought you might have some high-ranking prisoners we could interrogate," Alex said, getting right to the point.

"We had a similar idea and have been interrogating the officers that we have been capturing. Most have elected to join us, seeing the tide of the world shift. There is barely a UEDF troop on Earth anymore and the council is scattered. I had heard a report that Namgung committed suicide before being captured, Hernandez and Singh are both prisoners of the free men in Brazil and India. Kaufmann was killed by you," he said, pointing at William, "and Stahl was killed by the mob in New York."

"I take it Morgan and Moreau are hiding out?" William asked.

"Moreau came to our side, if you can believe it, which is how we got the information on where to find the others. No one has seen Morgan in several weeks, so she is probably hiding or off world."

"You are remarkably well informed, Commander," William commented.

"A lot has changed since you were last here. While you were busy fighting on the front lines all over the country, we got organized and used the communication stations we captured to share information. As it stands, we are winning, although we don't know if our enemies will receive reinforcements from the fleets orbiting Earth."

Concern flashed behind Weiss' eyes as he subconsciously glanced upward.

"Four of the five fleets are on their way to the colonies right now, trying to stop those planets from rebelling. They were sent several weeks ago. The 1st fleet is still up there, and I wouldn't be surprised if Harruhama is with it," Alex commented gravely.

"Earth has been on the edge of running out of many resources for a long time, he could just be waiting for the rebellion to lose steam before coming back or maybe he is giving up on Earth entirely, going for the colonies instead?" William questioned thoughtfully.

Alex cut in, the uncharacteristic edge of anger displayed on his face, "We won't know until we ask him directly."

"That could be difficult with the orbital defenses in place;

anything we try to send will be shot down by the grid, or by the 1st fleet," Weiss added.

"He can't be invincible, that fleet needs to be resupplied from Earth too. They can't stay up there forever," one of the other men offered.

"Either way, we need more information. I just might be able to get it," Alex declared. Looking at William he continued, "We may need to split up for a little while."

"Tell me the plan then, let's make sure we think it through and use every resource we have," William stated, staring at his stepson.

CHAPTER 5

Return to Station Sigma

A LATE-SUMMER STORM BLEW HEAVY WINDS ACROSS the plains outside Des Moines where Alex and William had stayed in an abandoned farm house just outside the city, a short drive from the free men headquarters. They had spent a few days making plans and thinking through contingencies for ending the war.

There hadn't been any fighting in the area since before they had arrived and a big part of both of them enjoyed the quiet time to catch up and exchange stories. William had been moving around a lot better with as much rest as they got since escaping from San Francisco and Alex didn't feel as bad leaving him to go on his mission.

The sound of the wind against the shuttered window woke him up before dawn and, not for the first time in the last few days, Alex's stomach was grumbling as he got out of bed. Food had become scarce and was heavily rationed.

The bed, however, had been the softest thing he had slept on in as long as he could remember and, though it was a nice change in some ways, it had made it difficult to fall asleep. For some reason he thought of Lyria in her apartment on Aeris VII sleeping on a soft bed. He had no idea what her bed was like but, because her skin and hair were soft, Alex imagined that her bed was too.

As he performed his morning stretches, Alex thought a lot about the girl that had captured his heart. He missed her. Though it only seemed like he had been gone a few weeks to him, to her he had been gone nearly two months. He regretted now that he didn't ask about her when he had talked to his Mom, but he had been so moved by William and Marlena's reunion that it didn't cross his mind at the time.

Before he could finish his routine, the smell of coffee and bacon made his stomach growl again so we made his way downstairs. The pictures of strangers that littered the wall bore quiet witness to the young man's steps as he walked swiftly to the kitchen where William was making breakfast.

"Coffee?" William asked, not turning around.

"Yeah, thanks," he replied as William poured the dark liquid.

"What are you doing up so early?" Alex asked, taking the offered mug.

"You've been getting up early every day, figured I'd make you breakfast before you left," the man replied over the sound of the storm outside, rattling the windows.

They had decided the night before that they couldn't afford to wait any longer and that Alex would set off in the morning.

"Thank you," Alex offered, drinking his coffee. "I'm going to be back, you know."

William turned and smiled at Alex. "Yes, I know you will."

"Then why are you worried?" he pushed, sensing concern.

"Not worried, just focusing. We both have a long road ahead and quite frankly, I've enjoyed the part of it that we travelled together."

"I wish you had a spaceship and could come with me, William. It would be a lot easier with you there," Alex offered.

"I'll try to make enough of a ruckus down here to keep their eyes off you as long as I can," the man replied absently, pulling a plate down from the cabinet and sliding the food onto it.

William served a few eggs, toast, and several slices of bacon to Alex and began cleaning up the kitchen.

"Where did you get all this food?" Alex trilled as he ravenously began to eat.

"Figured you'd need your strength more than me, plus, I'm heading out soon to raid a supply depot a few towns over that they missed. That's the last of the rations."

"Well eat some of the toast at least, I can't finish all this," Alex lied, moving his plate to share with William.

William saw through the ruse, but the two ate together anyway, enjoying the rhythmic sound of rain outside and the hearty meal.

When they had finished Alex went back upstairs, changed out of the civilian clothes he had been wearing, and dressed in his flight suit. He noted with a grin that several of the small tears it had accumulated had been mended. He didn't have any other possessions to take with him so with a glance back at the uncomfortably soft bed, he went back downstairs to find William dressed in his duster and waiting.

Sharing a brief hug, they let a moment pass before speaking.

"It was really good to see you," Alex started.

"You too, Alex. Let's end this war, so we can get back to the important stuff," William smiled.

With a chuckle and one last look back, Alex walked out into the rain.

He trotted from the house to the barn, where Skoll sat waiting. In one deft move, he leapt up and into the suit, feeling the familiar compression of the hatch closing behind him. He was soon looking through the eyes of the machine. At the front door of the house, William watched him go, beaming with pride.

Moments later, Skoll walked out into the yard, crouched for a moment, then leapt into the sky, the thrusters on its legs and back lighting up the predawn morning at the farm. Upwards it flew into the clouds where the orange glow quickly faded from sight, followed by the strange popping noise of an in atmosphere slipstream.

After Alex was gone, William took a deep breath and walked back inside the house and gathered the rest of his gear. He packed quickly and, without looking back, left the farm.

—

Skoll arrived moments later surrounded by darkness, easily moving into a high orbit around Mars. Alex took a few moments to get used to the orientation of space and the lack of gravity before beginning to scan.

His eyes flashed over his sensors, *no enemy ships.*

"Good, now where are you sigma?" he mumbled.

It took nearly an hour of moving against orbit before the station came into sensor range. The battle station that had been Alex's home for over a year appeared much smaller than he remembered it as it careened over the horizon.

"Station Sigma, this is transport vessel A6117 bringing cargo and food from Earth, is anyone there, over?" he hailed, using the fake credentials he and William thought up.

No response.

Alex's forehead furrowed, confused. He tried hailing again. Nothing.

Scanning the station, he noted that none of the escape pods had been jettisoned, nor were there any ships attached to the facility.

"Okay, what's going on?"

Picking the cargo bay that he had originally exited from before the mission to the Eagle Nebula, Alex used the strong hands of Skoll to force open the doors, active force shielding kept oxygen from escaping as he entered the station.

"The lights are on, at least," he mused.

Still inside his battle suit vessel, Alex began to scan the station around him. His motion sensor flared to life with the movement of several large groups in different parts of the station.

He tried accessing the security system cameras.

System disabled.

"Weird, okay. I guess I have to go see."

Alex exited his ship, landing on the ground easily, and moved quickly to the door of the cargo bay. Through the neuro-sync, Alex kept the image of his motion sensor in the corner of his vision.

Detecting no motion anywhere near him, he exited into the narrow hall and began to head toward the command center, where the largest group was located.

He moved as quickly as he could, sacrificing stealth for speed, realizing that if anyone still on the station had an OMBI, they probably already knew where he was.

As he got within sight of the door to the command center, a voice called out.

"Who is that down there?" the male voice shouted.

"Captain Pereira from Black Squadron!" Alex shouted back, not stopping his approach.

"Liar, Mephisto died in the Eagle Nebula!"

"Nope, just look at me! I am definitely alive," Alex called out flippantly, recognizing the voice.

"Are you with us then? Or are you with the others?"

The boy was nervous. Alex slowed, reaching through his OMBI to raise his shield.

"I just got here and I don't know what's going on, but if you don't shoot me, I'll be glad to listen," Alex offered, raising his hands.

The worried face of Anthony Ramirez looked back at him from the slightly open door.

"Hi, Slayer." Alex waved.

"Hi, Mephisto. You can come in, but don't try anything and don't be stupid about shooting. This close to the outer hull, no one shoots, it's all Melee weapons," Slayer chided hesitantly.

Inside the command center, Alex looked around at many familiar faces. The entirety of Blue Army 2121 and 2122 rimmed the circular room, talking in small groups along with most of Black Army 2122. Colonel Lemmon was lying on a makeshift cot, babbling incoherently, a bloodstained bandage wrapped tightly around his head.

"What happened?" Alex asked his Blue Army counterpart, pointing around the room of half-starved kids.

"We had an early graduation, as things were getting bad on Earth. They even graduated the 2122 class," Slayer explained. "They sent both Red Squadrons to Earth first but the engineer made a mistake and damaged my 4th inhibitor while removing my 2nd. He said they couldn't fix it and then that idiot tried to pull a gun on me! I had to kill him, Mephisto."

"Oh man. What happened then?" Alex prodded.

"As Blue Army came in, I jacked an AFMR and had it remove all their 4th inhibitors. We went to the Black Army barracks after that, and talked them into joining us. By then, the rest of the base was on high alert. That's when Colonel Lemmon found us, and brought us to the command center. He was helping us before he got hurt."

"So the others you mentioned are Yellow and Green? Why are they attacking?"

"Some sub-commander from the fleet ordered all the station troops to subdue us and got to them first. They tried to take the command center but we held them off. We managed to shut down the security and communication systems after that. It's all melee fighting and arrows since then. No one wants to risk a hull breach," Slayer finished.

"It looks like you haven't had many casualties," Alex offered, inspecting the one hundred or so people in the room.

"Neither have they, it's become a big waiting game. They have the food, but can't get off the station. We are running low on food, but control all the systems. By the way, what are you doing here? We heard you died."

Alex took a deep breath and explained everything about Black Squadron, his mom, the rebellion on Earth, and the colonies as concisely as he could. Slayer and the other members of Blue and Black armies listened intently. He ended by telling them what the 4th inhibitors did and how the UEDF had been altering their perceptions.

"I have my battle suit vessel in a docking bay," Alex finished, half kidding. "I could go punch a hole in the side of the station on their side and end this conflict pretty quickly."

Slayer paled.

"Uh, let's call that plan B. They aren't bad, they are being manipulated. Even the soldiers on the station probably don't know the truth. We need to beat them, but try to help as many of them as possible. If we are going to join the fighting we want as many OMBI soldiers as we can get, right?"

"You've changed, man. Alright, Let's do it that way; it looks like we have about a hundred hungry soldiers, Green and Yellow classes would be about one-sixty, plus what, three hundred or so soldiers?" Alex asked, doing the math in his head.

"That's pretty much correct, we're badly outnumbered and a lot of our guys are weak from hunger," Slayer agreed.

"Four to one? Connor could do it," Alex muttered under his breath, remembering hearing about Connor's victory from Major Sanders against similar odds.

"I'm glad you're here to help us." Slayer extended his hand to Alex.

Alex shook the boy's hand briefly. The two walked over to

the control panel and began going over the station layout. The station was round with many docking bays and cargo holds along the outer corridor. The command center was on the outside as well. There were many corridors leading inward all around the ship like a wagon wheel, toward the training rooms, barracks, medical facility, commissary, and armory. The situation was good for escape, if there were ships to escape in and bad for advancement, as the hall narrowed down to a few corridors into only a few fortified areas.

The motion sensor readings were encouraging though. OMBI soldiers didn't appear to associate with station troops much, and Yellow and Green armies were spread out among the four areas, apparently growing comfortable with their greater numbers.

Nodding to Colonel Lemmon, Alex asked, "Is he going to be okay?"

Slayer shook his head. "He needs an AFMR, but all the working ones left are on the other side of the station."

"Okay well, I need his help when we get this figured out, so let's work on that first. Besides, if their commander were conscious, some of those three hundred troops might give up," Alex articulated thoughtfully.

"That's a good idea. Medical isn't really well guarded, not like the armory and commissary." Slayer nodded.

"I will attack their main force head on while you and a few of your best guys get that AFMR," Alex suggested.

"What?" Slayer shuddered. "That's suicide!"

Alex smirked. "Nah, I got it. They won't even touch me. I'll just go create a diversion and get out of there. I don't want them looking at their motion sensors when you guys raid Medical. Make sure you grab all the supplies you can. If I can get some food, I will."

"You're crazy, you know that, right?" Slayer stammered, despite Alex's reputation for being undefeated.

Alex just smiled as he closed his eyes, taking seven deep breaths.

—

His footsteps echoed as he stalked down cold gray halls of station sigma, feeling his heart pound in his chest. Alex didn't feel too good about using non-lethal weapons against overwhelming numbers that would, no doubt, be shooting to kill. He quietly wished that he had access to a 2nd inhibitor chip to make all of his weapons non-lethal for this battle, but let the musing pass as he got close.

"Strike hard and fast," Alex reminded himself, wondering if maybe he was indeed crazy.

Going through his mental OMBI menu, it occurred to him that he had few non-lethal options available and none of the auto drones or vehicles would be much help in the narrow corridors. He was pretty good with his fists but he had only trained up to the master level and he was pretty sure at least a few of the other students in the opposing armies had reached that level too.

"Screw it," he cursed quietly, raising his armor and shields.

The door on the far end of the hall was shut. The red-lettered "Commissary" sign slightly flickered as Alex began to run.

Using the enhanced strength and speed of his OMBI, Alex leapt at the sealed door and threw his weight against it in a double kick. The boy proved stronger than the steel and the door blew from its hinges into a waiting trio of armed Yellow Army troops.

"Figures it'd be Yellow," Alex mused as he noted the heavy fortifications around the room.

He silently thanked his luck. Green Army was known for

setting traps and breaking rules, a fact he resolved to remember the next time he charged recklessly into a room full of enemies.

He spun from the ground onto his feet, manifesting a long staff, which he spun menacingly around his body, keeping the surprised Yellow Army soldiers at bay. With a quick glance, Alex realized how desperately outnumbered he was.

Weapons began manifesting the waiting hands of trained OMBI Soldiers. Alex dove toward a pair of younger soldiers as their swords manifested, knocking away their weapons quickly and slamming his staff into each of their heads with a quick motion.

The crack of metal on bone caused him to wince slightly as the pair crumbled to the ground. His momentum quickly spent, Alex watched armor begin appearing on the remaining forces.

Moving quickly to engage another group of five, Alex kept things close, not giving the soldiers with ranged weapons an open shot.

"Forget the guns, get in there and get him," he heard one boy call out.

Unfortunately for Yellow Army, Alex excelled at this kind of fight, having been outnumbered many times in the battle arenas. He didn't know how to lose. Falling into a rhythm, he let his instincts guide his body as he split his staff in two, the ends igniting into flashing, electrical arcs.

"That's new," he grinned, realizing as he stunned the boy next to him that he had subconsciously unlocked a non-lethal weapon.

The weapon proved useful against the metallic armor and weapons his enemies used. Every blocking sword resulted in a satisfying grunt as the wielder fell away.

Alex dodged around the swinging axe of a large boy, rolling forward into a double strike against a surprised spear wielder. The kid went down in a heap, gyrating on the floor.

"Well this is going well," Alex quipped as he spun to avoid another swing from the boy with the axe.

He received a scratch on his armor as he rolled away. Several more scratches followed from weapons he couldn't completely avoid as the soldiers from Yellow Army swarmed him.

Only six were down when the enemies began to surround him. As surprise wore off, the attackers struck out with measured strikes of longer weapons, not letting him make progress in any direction.

"Surrender or die!" one soldier yelled, drawing a chuckle from Alex.

The circle of enemies moved with him, keeping their distance and prodding at him with spears, which he tapped with electrical energy, causing the wielders to back off a bit. He tried to move the circle toward the tables in the room, but had trouble getting the enemies to respond right.

Alex grimaced as a spear caught his side, causing his armor in that area to evaporate. To his dismay, reinforcements from Green Army began entering the room, although they seemed content to stay back and yell encouragement from the walls around the commissary.

"Get that lizard!" Yellow Army's commander yelled.

Alex laughed despite the dire situation and wondered how inhibitor chips knew he was an enemy.

Suddenly the door on the far end opened and UEDF troops burst in.

"We need backup in the med bay!" one shouted.

"Time to go," Alex barked.

He clapped his weapons together three times, causing a build-up of flashing electrical energy. He quickly dissipated his metal armor and jumped up into the air, twisting and dodging as he merged the stunning batons into one large staff again. He slammed the floor with the tip, pushing himself up so his feet were against the ceiling.

He released the stored electrical energy into the metal floor in one surge, causing the lights in the room to flicker and the soldiers to stagger. The innermost kids flew back into the outer ring.

Using the distraction, Alex let his weapon dissipate and ran to a nearby pantry, where he grabbed the first bag that he saw.

He flung the bag into a soldier that followed him in, knocking him to the ground. He grabbed the bag on his way out, running out into the hallway as fast as his OMBI-enhanced legs would carry him.

Not detecting any pursuit, he slowed down a bit and walked the rest of the way back to the command center, out of breath and holding a sack of potatoes.

—

Slayer's attack on the medical center didn't go quite as well as Alex's attack on the commissary. Three of his ten soldiers were injured pretty badly and none had escaped unscathed. They had managed to recover an AFMR though, and as Alex walked into the room it was working to treat the wounds. When it finished, it had begun walking back toward the medical facility until Alex overrode the command and kept it in the command center.

The potatoes that Alex had grabbed didn't last very long as Blue and Black Army divided and ate them quickly. Colonel Lemmon was kept sedated, but he appeared to be breathing easier and was no longer bleeding after the AFMR worked on him.

Alex passed the time by talking to Slayer about what had happened since he left the station. Most of the other soldiers listened intently while taking turns watching their motion sensors and the hallway.

Days passed and hunger began to set in again before

Colonel Lemmon regained consciousness. Alex had hated the idle time, but he needed his old commander's help to get to General Harruhama.

He awoke slowly, unable to get his bearings.

Once he was awake, the AFMR inspected him and told him to continue to rest. Afterwards the machine moved to nearly every soldier, reminding them that they were malnourished and even began to recommend various types of food until they disabled its voice box.

"It's good to see that you're alive, Pereira," Lemmon began slowly. "I had heard that you were killed along with nearly all of your squadron."

Alex took a deep breath before explaining what happened, from the war in the colonies to the rebellion on Earth.

"I see, that explains a lot," Lemmon stammered after Alex had finished.

"I returned to Sigma to see if you could help me locate Harruhama."

"I have some thoughts on that, but we need to get this station secured first. What is the current situation?"

"Neither side is moving. Green and Yellow have most of the resources and have teamed up with the regular UEDF troops on the station. Now that you're awake, I don't think you'll be perceived as a Gortha, so maybe you can talk to them?"

Lemmon nodded as he reactivated the station communications.

"This is Colonel Lemmon, I order all personnel to stand down. Any soldier wearing an OMBI may be being deceived by a bug in the system. There are no Gortha on the station."

"Sir, it's good to hear your voice. We had thought you were taken by enemies," came the reply.

"I assure you I'm fine. Let's meet up and see if we can figure this out."

It took some convincing, but the hostile force eventually agreed to a negotiation. Being the only non-Gortha in the command center, Lemmon was invited to the barracks for a sit down with Yellow and Green Armies as well as the Sergeant in charge of the regular troops on the station. Alex went with him, promising no hostility. The AFMR followed quietly and eventually removed the inhibitor chips of the other armies.

It would have been a difficult sell to the OMBI soldiers alone, except as they talked to the sergeant about what he saw, it became obvious that they were being manipulated.

It took the better part of a day to remove all the 4th inhibitors and get the station back to running order. Unfortunately there were only escape pods and Skoll on the ship, otherwise Alex would have accepted the various requests of OMBI soldiers to go into battle on Earth.

When the station had settled down, Alex began to discuss his situation with Colonel Lemmon, telling him about the rebellion, his mother, and the corruption in the UEDF. Lemmon listened quietly while Alex spoke, the struggle between being a good soldier and a good man apparent on his face. The good man won in the end and Lemmon agreed to Alex's plan.

It was honest and simple enough, report directly to Harruhama that Alex had taken over Station Sigma and to send reinforcements. Then track the transmission back to the Nostus and find out where it was at so Alex could go there. As long as he didn't end up too close to the orbital defense grid around Earth while in a battle like before, he figured that he could board the ship.

So, without further prompting, Colonel Lemmon sent his report while Alex monitored it from Skoll.

The transmission went out, but there was no reply.

—

"Five minutes," he heard in his earpiece.

The morning light glittered off the English Channel as the low-flying transport cut through the air toward the last bastion of UEDF forces on Earth. The cool September air blew through the cabin as William and twenty special forces soldiers sat in rows, anxiously awaiting their mission.

The soldiers had defected along with Councilman Moreau right after his public apology for the people of Earth and the colonies. Then, to no one's surprise, he resigned from the UEDF and endorsed an elected civilian government to avoid execution.

The councilwoman from England was another story, however, as she represented the last of the UEDF's influence on Earth and had been rallying whatever troops remained to the UEDF in London. They would have been left alone, but the free men had intercepted a communication to the fleet in orbit, a request to bombard every major capital and for immediate reinforcements, which it had received nearly a week earlier from Station Sigma. It was decided unanimously among the leaders of the rebellion to use Moreau's information to capture Morgan if possible and prevent the dangerous OMBI soldiers from gaining a foothold on Earth.

William had insisted on joining the special forces team in the capture attempt while the military and free men forces attacked head on.

The mission was being documented and was to be broadcasted upon its success. The man who had defied the oppressive military regime alone and begun the rebellion was an icon that was too important to the legitimacy of the free men leaders who he had endorsed. He even gave the journalist permission to use his true identity after the mission was complete, now that his adopted children were out of the hands of the UEDF. The journalist was sitting across from William even then, writing the story of the husband who had lost his wife and had his children taken from him, fighting back against a tyrannical government.

William hadn't revealed to any of them yet that Marlena was alive, since the UEDF's betrayal was still a major motivation in the rebellion.

As the water gave way to land, the low transport followed the shoreline before turning inland while William reflected on the road that led to where he was at. The months of rebellion felt like years and the man was sure that he looked a lot older than when he had started on his campaign.

"Eyes up," someone said over the ear-piece.

William could see the distant battle out his window. The free men vastly outnumbered the defenders, but the eighty young OMBI soldiers with their versatile ability to change weaponry and summon vehicles and aircraft were attacking aggressively, pushing back the main forces.

The transport landed just outside the base's perimeter away from the main battle. William Mercer led the special forces unit, the journalist, and his videographer up to the steel wall.

Tiny discs of thermite from the under barrel of his shotgun sizzled into the wall, causing it to melt and split. After a minute, the team was inside the compound. They split into two teams; the first moved around the perimeter quietly, taking down sentries with their silenced weapons, securing the exit back to the transport. William's team moved toward the command center.

His legs, enhanced by his armor, carried him quickly ahead of the group to the back door, where two nervous guards paced anxiously. William didn't slow. Covering the distance in seconds, he dispatched the pair with two swings from the butt of his shotgun.

When his team arrived, William used his thermite launcher again, melting the hinges of the door. As it fell outward, he caught it and lowered it quietly to the ground.

Ahead of him his troops moved into a long hallway in pairs, covering each other's advance.

William signaled to the doors on the sides, sending his team in to clear the rooms. The first was empty. In the second a surprised man fell quickly to the experienced team.

Moving down the hall at a steady walking pace, his shotgun aimed in front of him, William found the communications center.

He opened the door quickly and his team moved in. Confused operators all but threw their hands toward the ceiling.

"Where is Morgan?" William asked one of the surrendering operators.

"A-at the end of the h-hall, in Operations," the man stammered.

"Shut down communications, let's go," William ordered the team as he exited back into the hall.

A piercing alarm blared in the building just before the charges could be set.

"Enemies have entered the base!" a voice cried.

At the end of the hall, the door to Operations opened and a teenage kid stepped into the hallway, his wrist glowing red.

Using his shotgun, William fired a barrage of explosive pellets forward from one barrel and immediately opened a hole in the wall beside him with the other. He didn't watch the pellets explode, but instead dove through the hole as a stream of machinegun fire erupted in the hallway behind him from both sides.

The special forces team broke apart, men diving for cover in all directions as the armored and shielded OMBI soldier walked slowly down the hall toward them, continuing his endless barrage of machinegun fire.

"How do we fight that?" one of the men screamed as he hid in the communications room.

William pulled the pins on two of the grenades he had on his belt, counted to three, and threw them down the hall. The explosion shook the building and, as William walked into the hallway, the force of the blast blew his duster backwards and almost knocked the black cowboy hat off his head.

The Red Squadron OMBI soldier was dazed but not down and William fired a double barrel barrage of explosive pellets, charging down the hall and attacking the stunned kid as his armor dissipated. Through the smoke and debris, the OMBI soldier cried out, dashing forward with a long, thin blade.

Quick reactions, combined with enhanced movements, kept him from getting skewered as he managed to dodge, the blade getting caught up in his duster. Before he could release the manifestation, William slugged the kid in the stomach, knocking him to his knees. William winced as he slammed the butt of his shotgun into the side of the kid's head, knocking him to the floor.

Straightening his hat, William waved his team forward and shoulder charged into the door to Operations. The door buckled under the weight of the charge, opening to reveal a very surprised Councilwoman Morgan flanked by four armed bodyguards.

William scrambled behind a nearby table, covering his face as the machinegun fire tore through his coat into his battle armor. The armor absorbed most of the force of the bullets but they still stung as they tore through the wood of the table.

Soon the gunfire stopped as the special forces team eliminated the distracted bodyguards.

A soldier helped William to his feet and he walked unsteadily over to where Morgan was cowering in a corner.

"Please surrender and order your forces to stand down, Ms. Morgan. The UEDF is done," he said calmly, removing the bandana from his face.

The spark of recognition was immediate.

"I know you," Morgan said, her accent thick on her words. "You're that American architect."

"I am just a man who had his wife and stepsons taken from him by the UEDF, nothing more than that. No one else needs to go through that. We know the Gortha aren't real and the free men have been in contact with the colonies. The only attack they face is the UEDF fleets. They are willing to trade with Earth, but we need to pull together and take down the man responsible for the lies and the atrocities," he said, offering his hand.

"Harruhama," Morgan nodded, taking the man's hand, "he has been using the council as his puppets for years. I'm sorry for your loss, Mr. Mercer. I honestly have no idea how it has gotten so bad. But I want the fighting to stop too."

"Order your troops to lay down arms," William ordered, "and we will accept your surrender."

Councilwoman Morgan, in the last act of the UEDF council, walked over to her control panel and ordered the complete surrender of the UEDF troops on Earth.

~

On September 10th, 2121, exactly five months after his funeral, the UEDF troops on Earth surrendered to the Dragoon. The regular troops laid down their arms immediately when they received the order. The OMBI soldiers from Red Army were slower to stop fighting, but eventually, without the support of the UEDF, were forced to surrender as well.

There had been few casualties in the battle and the wounded were treated by the 311 AFMR that were brought in by both sides.

William personally led the former councilwoman back to the transport where they, and the Special Forces unit that had supported him, headed to a secure location to meet with commanders of the free men from all over the world in order to develop a plan on ridding Earth of the threat of the fleet looming in the atmosphere above them.

CHAPTER 6

An Unanticipated Reunion

A FOLD IN SPACE DISTORTED THE STARS DEEP IN THE Omega Nebula as Tizona emerged from the slipstream. Her eyes widened as she checked her navigation screen. Marlena had never emerged from a slipstream so close to her intended target before; she was a mere two hours away from Dytopa II. Warily she glanced over her shoulder toward her cargo bay, in the direction of the strange battle suit.

"Did you do that?" she whispered.

"What's that?" Artemis cut in.

"Never mind, we will be landing in a couple hours, make sure everything is ready," Marlena ordered as she tapped on the screen.

The twenty-day trip passed in a short two hours for the Tizona and her passengers. Anataur had slept through it while Artemis read a datapad, catching up on the events she had missed while she was a prisoner on Aeris VII. As the hazy brown planet that orbited a bright, white dwarf star came into view, Marlena set a course for Tiberius Falls and sent a message.

To: Dr. Arminus

Subject: OMBIcademy ship

Message: Doctor, this is Captain Mercer. We are arriving shortly. Please meet us at the spaceport, landing pad 4. My group is going on an expedition to the ship you discovered near the Scorpio Sea. Your assistance would be appreciated.

The Omega Nebula Colony had joined the Independent Colonies in the early days and Marlena hadn't been there since before there was a city. Her memories were fuzzy about the planet, but she did recall the landing site was above the fog layer that covered the planet. She noted that the frigates assigned to defend the colony were gone, having been called back to the capital.

Her communication device lit up when she was about an hour from landing, a recording from the scientific survey office.

"We are sorry to inform you that Dr. Miles Arminus went missing about a month ago when he went into a storm to gather data on the structure he discovered. His assistant has been informed of your arrival and will meet you at the landing pad, his name is Ethan Pereira."

Marlena froze as familiar numbness filled her chest at the sound of the man's name. Ethan had been her husband for ten years, but it had been eleven more since he had left, leaving a pregnant Marlena and five-year-old Alex, alone. She wasn't bitter about it, she had met William a year later and hadn't thought about Ethan much after that. Other than to occasionally wonder what happened the night he hadn't come home.

A sense of disdain filled her at the idea of the pending conversation when so much else was happening. She tried to steady herself, but found herself shaking. The following hour went by in a blur of old memories for Marlena, only being interrupted when Artemis tapped her on the shoulder, breaking her from her reverie.

"We're here," Artemis offered as she and Anataur moved to secure Connor's hovering tube from the cargo hold. Gathering a backpack of supplies and a sidearm, Marlena exited her ship to face a ghost.

The man standing on the gusty platform looked a lot like she remembered, except his brown hair had grown long and was unkempt, with an edge of gray appearing at his temples. His green eyes, which had lost their luster in his despair all those years ago, had gained some of it back. Even so, he carried himself with the telltale hardness of a man living on one of the more unforgiving colonies.

He stared back at her, as if he was trying to figure out the right tool for a complex job. It was apparent that he had not forgotten her fiery temper.

"This is a long way to go for milk, isn't it?" she finally quipped, breaking the tension.

Ethan smirked despite himself.

"Yeah well, the store down the street didn't have my brand, so…" he played along, still on edge, "I'm sorry."

His eyes were sincere, and his 6'2" frame seemed to diminish a bit. It was clear from the way he carried his shoulders that he had not forgiven himself, and in that moment Marlena remembered she hadn't held a grudge over it in a long time.

"Forget it. I forgave you a long time ago, Ethan," she said, almost feeling bad for him.

"How's Alex?" he asked suddenly, changing the subject.

"It's a long story, but he's doing okay. He is leading a rebellion on Earth with my husband, William," she replied, moving beside Connor's tube.

He flinched slightly.

"I hear you've been busy. I heard you died and then you got my colony to join the Independents and have been leading your own rebellion." He shook his head. "You always were a lot more than I ever deserved."

She laughed a bit at that and nodded.

"This is Connor, Alex's brother." She put her hand on the tube.

He looked a lot like Ethan, having similar eyes and hair. The man put his hand on the glass of the tube and repeated the boy's name to himself.

"What happened to him?" Ethan asked, the concern heavily in his voice.

"The device on his arm detonated. We think we can find a replacement in the ship you and Dr. Arminus discovered," she explained, eying Ethan.

Ethan nodded along thoughtfully. "I'm not sure I understand how. I can get you there, if you can figure out how to open it. The storms are heavy right now, so we might have to wait a few months before…"

Her upraised hand caused him to stop.

"Just draw me a map. We can't wait for the storms to pass. We have a way in and will figure out the rest as we go," she ordered, her tone leaving no room for debate.

"Marlena, these storms are very dangerous. Are you sure it can't wait?"

"No, it can't," she retorted.

"It will be dark soon, at least start in the morning. I will take you there; the storms interfere with electronics, compasses and even a map wouldn't be much good to you. I have a non-electronic vehicle that will give us a decent chance at getting there in one piece and I know the way well enough. It will take about two days from here," he offered.

"That's fair," she said simply, taking her son back into her ship.

"I can find a place for you to stay…" he began.

"No, my quarters on my ship will be fine. But, you can put them up if you have the room." Marlena motioned to Artemis and Anataur.

He waved them to his open-topped truck.

"I'll be back at first light with the exploration rig. It's good to see you. I'm glad it all worked out okay," he said as he got behind the driver seat.

Without another word, he drove away with Artemis and Anataur.

Left to her thoughts, Marlena secured her cargo hold, checked on Connor's IV, and went to bed. Her dreams were troubled that night but she still awoke before dawn, forgoing breakfast to sit with her son in the cargo hold.

The others found her waiting impatiently when they arrived in a modified, six-wheeled AX-15 utility vehicle.

The two soldiers from Black Squadron loaded Connor's tube in the large cargo area in the back of the AX-15. Anataur got into the transparent pod at the top, which Ethan referred to as the "gunner's seat." Artemis sat in the cargo area with Connor, keeping his tube secure.

Marlena sat in the passenger seat while Ethan drove. Neither spoke much as they crawled through the windy streets of Tiberius Falls. The city had many structures that were built into the side of the mountain with tall towers, all of which had wind turbines on them. Although there were over two thousand colonists in the city, all of them lived on the top of the mountain, above the cloud line and the violent beast storms of Dytopa II.

—

Alex was lying in his old bunk, re-reading messages Connor had sent him while at the OMBIcademy, wondering how his mother was doing. He counted the days in his head and figured she was in the Omega Nebula somewhere and, not for the first time, thought about leaving the Sol system to go help his brother.

"I probably wouldn't make it on time anyway," he mumbled at no one in particular.

When he finished with the messages he started looking at pictures of Lyria he had saved to his OMBI. His heart fluttered as her face brightened up his virtual screen.

He thought about sending her a message but figured that, without the benefit of a data-slipstream, he would see her long before she ever got the message. He closed his eyes and imagined the way she felt as he kissed her, the smell of strawberry in her hair and the gentleness of her eyes when she smiled at him. The thought of her made him smile despite the ache in his heart.

He was still smiling when the alert appeared. Alex sprung from his bed and activated the console on the wall of his room to see three vessels approaching the station. He bolted from his room and down the long hall to the command center. Colonel Lemmon was already there when Alex arrived, looking carefully at the screen in front of him.

"Looks like two battle suits and a boarding transport." Lemmon explained, "It could be good; if we could capture that transport, we could get some troops down to Earth to assist the free men."

"Yeah, I guess," Alex said, half interested. He immediately went to studying the battle suits.

One was just the right size to be Fenris and Alex was eager for a rematch. The other gave Alex pause. It appeared to be larger or, at least, longer than Fenris.

"This could be rough," Alex murmured, running his hands through his hair.

"What's the plan?" Lemmon asked Alex, in an odd deferment of authority.

"Let them dock, I'd rather not fight three ships at once. Set an ambush in the docking bay for the transport ship and make sure we capture it. I'm not sure the battle suits will dock, but if they do I'll try to take down the pilots quickly," Alex explained while pointing at the monitor.

"One of them is Vertigo," Alex said simply, causing Lemmon to gasp.

"Are you going to be able to take out your friend?" the old Colonel asked, eying Alex with concern.

"Yeah, don't worry about it," Alex replied impassively.

Neither Fenris nor the other battle suit docked with the station, rather they flew around it menacingly. The transport did dock, but instead of troops, several 311 AFMR began to disembark with strange canisters on their backs.

The ambush team fell unconscious before they could make a report and the AFMR proceeded to walk around the station distributing the gas they carried, rendering the defenders unconscious before they could put up any resistance. Soldiers in hazard suits followed the AFMR out, putting bindings on the unconscious defenders and dragging them back into the transport.

Half the station fell before the command center got a reliable report of the nature of the attack. Lemmon began to hail the enemy ships, trying to get them to cease their attack, and Alex took a deep breath and ran as fast as he could to the cargo bay that held Skoll.

His lungs ached for air by the time he got to his ship. Having passed several of the AFMR, Alex didn't want to risk inhaling even once. Black spots had filled his vision by the time he boarded and the seal locked. He took several gasping breaths in order to remain conscious.

Acting on instinct, Alex punched in the codes to open the airlock and turned Skoll to face a giant winged serpent and the hulking form of Fenris.

Skoll reacted to Alex's thoughts and began unlocking several weapons on his OMBI. Cannons manifested on Skoll's strong arms as well as a shoulder-mounted launcher.

Alex smirked as the new weapons appeared.

He willed his battle suit into action and Skoll burst from the cargo hold of Station Sigma right between the enemy ships before they could react. Clearing the station, Skoll spun and unleased several small missiles from his shoulder and charged the arm cannons, firing a beam at Fenris.

An opaque shield became visible as the beam blasted into the larger ship. The shield visibly weakened, but held as Fenris returned fire with its own cannon.

The missiles that began chasing the serpent ship swirled through the darkness, following the strange swerving flight. The strange ship released counter measures, which sprayed brightly against the starry backdrop, causing the missiles to detonate quietly in the vacuum of space.

Alex didn't have much trouble keeping ahead of Vertigo's slower ship and hit it with another arm cannon beam before the serpent slithered toward him, quicker than he could follow. It moved erratically, changing speed and direction constantly, making it almost impossible to target. It didn't seem to have any weapons, but Alex tried to stay away from it as it closed the distance.

He raised his shields and his own armor, weaving and changing his own speed often to try to disorient his opponents. When the two separated, he manifested his twin blades and charged back into Fenris, slashing hard against dark armor and dancing away before he could be hit by the serpent as it came around behind him. The dance went on for a few minutes, Alex gaining momentum in the fight. He begun inflicting regular damage to the larger ship while avoiding the other ship he wasn't sure what to do about yet.

As he came in for another attack against the weakening Fenris, his old friend surprised him with a new trick. His hands manifested two sheathes, which absorbed Alex's twin swords when they connected. Following through with the motion as

Alex dissipated his scimitars, Fenris burst forward faster than Alex thought possible and shoulder slammed him back, causing his armor to weaken.

He wasn't stunned long, but the serpent came in fast, slamming into him astern, and began wrapping itself around him. Alex struggled to get Skoll's arms free but Fenris laid into him with several hits from his sword, causing Alex to focus on keeping his armor up rather than fight off the strange snake.

His body tensed as he felt Skoll strain against the squeezing of the enemy ship. Alex was trapped and, worse, the snake's armor began to lock in place, keeping Skoll from moving at all.

Alex let his weapons dissipate and stopped struggling against the squeeze. As his adrenaline faded, he began to feel instantly tired. He had not planned on being captured but, as he stopped fighting back, the squeezing seemed to lessen and Fenris hadn't made any move to attack him.

As Alex focused on the enemy ships, he could almost discern the pattern between them. They were communicating and Alex's skill with the OMBI almost had him hearing what they were saying when the familiar distorting of space began around him. They were slipstreaming.

—

The orange sky above the serene mountains of Dytopa II disappeared behind the dense cloud layer that sat a couple thousand feet below Tiberius Falls. Rare metals and minerals were abundant in the mountains, and before they reached the cloud-line Marlena saw many glittering deposits of strange gems and ore from the road. The colony thrived on those metals, living in the cold mountain air.

The landscape was vastly different inside the clouds. Where there was sparse vegetation in the sun, now sat monstrous trees and a lush landscape. Condensation began to build on the window of the AX-15 but it beaded and rolled off without affecting visibility much. What did decrease visibility was the dense, cold fog that moved slowly through the jungle around them.

"It's going to get difficult and slow from here. There are only a few months out of the year that this area is clear for us to explore, so the roads don't get maintained well," Ethan explained, his eyes intent on the fog ahead.

It wasn't long after that that their progress was halted by a large tree that had fallen in the roadway. The thick log stood taller than the AX-15, but Anataur popped open the bubble and hopped out of the gunner seat, manifesting a staff with a whirling sawblade at one end.

"It might not be the best tool for this, but I think I can remove the log," Anataur called out to the others.

Ethan got out of the vehicle too, grabbing the rifle from the rack behind his seat and loading it carefully.

"That noise could attract mist wolves. They are large, aggressive predators, best to stay in the vehicle," he said, looking at Marlena.

Despite the warning, she got out and climbed up to the gunner's seat of the AX-15, watching the forest intently. Ethan climbed onto the hood of the vehicle and fished a pair of strange-looking goggles from his belt pouch, putting them on.

Responding to Marlena's questioning stare, he said, "They give me thermal vision. The fog is warm compared to the hide of a mist wolf. It's not easy to spot them, but I've gotten pretty good at it working in the scientific research department."

She only nodded, looking back at the forest, unsure of exactly what to look for without the benefit of experience or thermal goggles.

As Anataur began his cutting, the grinding sound of metal on wood dissipated quickly in the dense fog but still caused a flock of strange, translucent birds to fly from the area. Sawdust began to accumulate on the boy's black flight suit as he worked, squinting against the thick dust.

Artemis exited the AX-15's cargo hold out the rear door and walked around the vehicle to watch Anataur work. She knew better than to criticize his cuts and was content to observe the work, even leaping up onto the fallen tree and walking down the remaining stump, disappearing into the fog. Ethan watched her through his goggles as she inspected the stump, returning a moment later.

"This tree was left here intentionally. You don't have a problem with fog bandits or whatever, do you?" she yelled over the sound of cutting.

"Who ever heard of bandits on a colony? And no, no one lives below the cloud line," he yelled in response.

It was a good point. The colonies were well known for honest, hard workers and had very little crime. As such, the amount of lawyers, judges, and law enforcement on any of the colonies was remarkably low. Most had a sheriff or leader of some sort that mitigated disputes. But out in the colonies, you earned what you had.

"Then who would want to block a road below the cloud-line?" Artemis asked.

Ethan opened his mouth to answer, but didn't get the chance. A strange piercing cry echoed over the saw cuts, sending shivers down Marlena's spine. The call was answered by several others on the opposite side of the vehicle, causing Ethan to whip his head from side to side. He pulled the slide on his rifle back and pressed the weapon against his shoulder, aiming out into the forest beyond.

"Get ready!" he called. "Mist wolves are hard to see in the fog but will only attack if they think we're vulnerable! If we can wound their alpha they'll probably disperse. Don't let one bite you though, their venom will paralyze you, permanently."

In response to Ethan's warning, Anataur stopped his sawing and manifested black body armor while shifting his vision from infrared to thermal. The saw dissipated and a large hammer appeared in his strong hands as he stood between the log and the AX-15, facing the right. Artemis stood beside him, watching the other way, black armor covering her lithe form as her eyes took on the white glow of her OMBI's thermal vision function. Her bow materialized soon after.

Ethan fired the first shot from his long rifle into the forest on the driver side of the vehicle, causing a wailing cry from the gray fog beyond. He pulled back the slide and loaded another long shell from his belt, where dozens more waited for him.

"You got one!" Artemis called, witnessing the hit.

"I barely wounded it, we should get out of here! This is a whole pack, not just the pathfinders!"

To emphasize his point, more wailing cries echoed all around them, sounding too close for comfort.

The brush on the right side of the vehicle moved as something large ran through it, faster than Marlena's eyes could follow. She tried to turn the heavy gun mounted on top of the AX-15 to track the target, but the turret was too slow.

Ethan fired another shot into the woods, causing a yelp followed by a large crashing sound in the brush.

"How big are these mist wolves?" Marlena yelled, feeling the vehicle wobble as one went down in the forest.

"Big," was all Ethan replied, while loading another shell into his rifle.

Artemis sent forth out a stream of arrows, drawing and firing in a blur of motion. She had no quiver, the arrows appeared as she pulled the string back, but the girl made a circular motion with her hand as if she were drawing from a quiver on her back. The arrows thudded upon impact, striking into the center of several trees.

Her intention was made clear when a large form passed between two of the trees and got wrapped up in a fine cord, which flashed with bluish electrical pulses and wrapped itself around the mist wolf. Stunned, the mist wolf's momentum carried it to the edge of the rough road where Marlena finally got a look at it.

The thing was massive, about the size of a rhinoceros on Earth, and had long fangs protruding from its upper jaw. Its coat appeared to be made of smoke, wafting off its body and dissipating into the fog at the ends, making it nearly invisible from even a short distance. What impacted Marlena the most was the thing's eyes, tight black beads of wild anger, staring right at her as it thrashed against the binding cord.

"Anataur, hammer this as hard as you can!" Artemis cried, loading an arrow with what looked like an axe head on it. She fired the strange arrow into the center of the log that blocked the road, next to where Anataur had been cutting.

Trusting his friend, Anataur lifted his large hammer and spun in a circle, building momentum before swinging hard into the arrow. The axe head bit deeply into the wood, almost all the way to the center of the great tree.

"Everyone get inside, now!" Artemis yelled, running to the rear of the vehicle. Marlena remained in the gunner seat while Anataur jumped into the passenger side. Ethan shouldered his rifle and jumped down from the hood, getting into the driver seat.

"Back up a bit," Artemis ordered.

Ethan did as commanded, pushing the gas pedal, sending the truck back until he slammed into something. The truck lurched and Marlena looked back to see what must have been the alpha mist wolf.

Screaming, she began firing the AX-15's main gun.

The large bullets seemed to pass right through the massive

beast, disappearing in the smoke of its coat. The huge wolf turned at her with terrible black eyes and howled so loud that Marlena didn't hear the log explode behind her as Artemis' explosive detonated.

The log split neatly, sending the two halves into the fog. With a hole large enough to drive through, Ethan stomped his foot on the gas, speeding deeper into the mists.

The alpha-wolf gave chase, snarling as its pack formed around it. Marlena only heard the muffled pops of gunfire over the ringing of her ears as she continued to shoot the AX-15's gun. Bullets from the main gun slashed through their misty coats, earning yelps, and, eventually, the pursuit dissipated.

A short time later Ethan slowed down and Marlena could hear again.

"We have a long way to go, still," Ethan explained, seeming unshaken by the encounter. "It's good you brought such resourceful soldiers."

Accepting the compliment, Anataur and Artemis both nodded, though both still glanced around nervously.

"We should be out of the mist in a couple hours. We'll set up camp there, provided there are no other surprises," he stated.

"Uh, camp? Isn't it a little dangerous to camp with those things so close?" Anataur asked, his voice shaking as he peered out into the fog.

"Mist wolves won't go near the bottom of the cloud-line. They are far too afraid of what is on the other side." Ethan said it casually, but the other three members of the team all paled at the idea of what could possibly scare a mist wolf.

CHAPTER 7

Calm Before the Storm

LEX AWOKE FROM A DREAMLESS SLEEP STILL INSIDE Skoll. As he blinked the sleep from his eyes, he found himself staring up at the ceiling of a docking bay. He didn't remember what happened after the slipstream, but found that as he tried to move, he could feel the straps around Skoll as if they were pressing into his own flesh. Skoll's shoulders were propped up against something that Alex couldn't see.

"Okay, you got me," Alex said coolly.

"He is awake, sir," Alex could hear someone say over an unexpectedly open comm channel.

"Get him out of his ship and down to the detention area," another voice replied.

Alex took a deep breath and opened the rear hatched of his ship, closing it behind him as he slipped out. His legs were wobbly, and the fuzziness in his head kept him from manifesting any weapons or armor. He could, however, hear and feel the electronics around him better somehow, as if they were all trying to tell him a story. In his haze, he could hear them like he never could before.

The sound of heavy boots stole the thought from him as Vertigo and several armed UEDF soldiers approached.

"Not bad fighting out there. If you hadn't been gassed on

Sigma, you might have won," Vertigo remarked with admiration. "There is something I don't understand though, why is it when you board your battle suit vessel, does it become a Gortha ship? What did they do to you?"

Alex winced at the sincerity of the question. He knew that his friend wasn't dumb and though he had remained loyal to the UEDF when Alex defected to the rebels, he really couldn't fault him for it. He clearly believed that the Gortha were still real and that Alex had been mind-controlled during the battle of the Eagle Nebula.

"You probably won't believe it, because you still have your 4th inhibitor, but the Gortha aren't real, Austin. When you removed my inhibitor, I saw the truth. My mom is alive and we were fighting her and colony ships, only we were tricked so we couldn't see them," Alex explained.

The guards grabbed Alex roughly and pushed him toward the door.

"Even if what you say is true, Alex, you're still AWOL and joined an enemy faction!" Austin yelled, his face contorting with rage.

"Yeah, that's true," Alex admitted.

They didn't speak any more as Alex was escorted down the gray halls of the ship toward the detention area.

"Where am I anyway?" Alex asked.

"Shut up, that's where," a particularly snarky guard replied, which actually made Alex chuckle despite the circumstances.

The same guard forced Alex into his cell roughly and slammed the door shut.

—

A camp flare burned inside a ring of rocks, its light kept cautiously contained. The cloud-line loomed above like a low ceiling as Ethan cooked upon a small stove. A distant howl from the clouds above cut the night air and forced a chill down Marlena's spine as she absently picked at her ration bar. She imagined the mist wolf pack hunting down some other horrible monstrosity as more howls answered the first in a mournful song.

"That sound..." she muttered.

"I know," Ethan replied, staring at the fire.

Her eyes followed the road as she looked out over the moon-lit valley. Mountains jutted from grassy planes into the clouds at regular intervals and gave way to barren hills that fell away into grassy plains. The landscape was divided by a ravine that many tall trees grew out of. Even at night, the valleys of Dytopa II were warm, causing Marlena to sweat beneath her battle suit.

The sky was illuminated slightly with an orange tint as a fire burning somewhere beyond where she could see left a layer of heavy smoke that didn't go above the clouds.

"We're lucky," Ethan said, following her gaze out into the plains. "It's a calm evening. It gets bad when the winds pick up and the storm begins; stirs the beasts."

"What kind of beasts are out there, that something like a mist wolf is afraid of it?" she whispered, feeling her heart pound.

She had heard stories of the Dytopa II storms, but even among the colonists, most people didn't know what was below the cloud-line.

"I haven't spent a lot of time down here during the storms, only once when our recon mission went too long. We did everything we could to get back as quickly as possible and didn't linger. We haven't identified all the species, but the rift tiger is the one that gives us the most trouble when we cross, normally. It has six legs and is very fast, smart, a lot bigger than a mist wolf. It's one of the more difficult creatures to deal with, since it doesn't follow the storm," Ethan said, staring blankly toward the plains.

"That sounds terrifying, what else is out there?" she asked, not taking her eyes from the valley.

"A lot of things I hope we don't come across. Some of the birds out there can lift up smaller vehicles and are pretty hard to hit with my rifle. I once saw an arachni-bear, but it was eating the corpse of something big and ignored us."

Artemis and Anataur had stopped their conversation and were staring at Ethan intently.

"What is an arachni-bear?" Anataur asked, rubbing his hands together anxiously.

"It's a stupid name that I gave it, it looks like a bear with eight legs and a spider's face. They make webs to catch larger beasts and then swarm them. We probably won't see one. Even in the storms they prefer the ravines and we aren't going down there. The ship that I am taking you to is in the side of a mountain on the far side of the plains, by the Scorpio Sea," he said, pointing out into the distance.

"I don't see the sea," Anataur commented.

The shaking in his voice drew a pat on the shoulder from Artemis.

"Well, it's hazy and dark, but it's out there. Not exactly close. It will be a dangerous crossing, like I said. I've never been down here during the middle of storm season," Ethan said, taking the cooking pot off the fire.

"Where do the beasts go when the storms are gone?" Anataur asked, enthralled.

"I asked Dr. Arminus the same thing. His guess was that they were somehow allergic to too much sunlight and live underground when the storms are gone. There is a popular rumor that this planet is mostly hollow and full of creatures that live in the dark, only occasionally stirred up by the storms."

"Are you trying to scare them?" Marlena asked, trying to keep the fear out of her own voice.

"No, but they should be scared and so should you. I'm scared! I have seen what's out there," he cautioned, waving a ladle toward her.

Ethan began serving a savory-smelling stew into bowls and passing them out.

"Well, I'm sleeping in the truck," Anataur announced suddenly, heading inside without eating.

Artemis chuckled, accepting a bowl. They ate in silence until she broke the silence.

"I've got first watch," she said suddenly, hopping onto the hood of the AX-15.

Ethan nodded to Artemis and set up a yellow-tinted force bubble around himself, settling in for the night.

Artemis flipped through her OMBI menus until she caught Marlena's questioning glance.

"Motion tracker, night vision, force shield, and in a minute, trip wire alarms," she said with a shrug.

Marlena smiled as she nodded before heading into the cargo hold and putting her pillow on the bench seat next to Connor's tube.

"I don't care what's out there. I won't let anything stop me from helping you, my sweet baby boy," she said, placing her hand on the thick glass.

She fell asleep there, with her head next to the glass, where she could faintly hear the rhythmic snoring of her youngest son.

———

Marlena awoke several times during the night to the sound of crashing trees in the clouds above and strange animal calls from the plains below. The night was dark and she couldn't see anything when she looked out the small windows in the back of the AX-15, beyond the strange orange glow.

As it was getting light outside she was awoken by the noise of thunder, which caused the entire vehicle to shake. Ethan was packing up his supplies and Artemis sat vigilantly on the hood, looking in all directions.

"You didn't sleep?" Marlena asked with concern as she exited the AX-15.

"No, I'll sleep while we drive, I figured the driver and the gunner should be well rested before heading down there. Also, no offense, but you seemed like you needed it," Artemis explained.

Artemis took Anataur's cot inside the vehicle while the broad-shouldered boy manned the heavy machine gun. Ethan loaded his equipment quietly, lost in thought.

"We should get there tonight," he said to Marlena as she got into the passenger seat, "if we don't get delayed too much by the storm."

"Are you okay?" Marlena asked, reading his expressions. "What's on your mind?"

"Oh, it's all still a little difficult to swallow is all. You, Connor, this mission." He shrugged off her concern.

"What else is it? You've been kind of quiet since we fought those wolves."

He paused a moment before starting the vehicle.

"That tree. My last time through there was nothing in the way, but that tree had been put there on purpose. Dr. Arminus went missing a month ago. He never left without me, Marlena. They told me he went into the storm alone and just never came back. I wonder if maybe it was him who cut the tree," Ethan explained.

"Sorry. I didn't think of that. Maybe we will find him when we get to the ship." Marlena shrugged.

Ethan shrugged back and started the AX-15.

"Everyone stay alert today, this is new to me and I am not

sure what to expect," he called as they began moving down into the plains.

They rolled slowly down what was left of the dirt road, going over bumps that occasionally lifted Marlena from her seat. Making the ride more uncomfortable, the wind howled and buffeted the vehicle to the side violently. Ethan drove with both hands on the wheel, his knuckles white and forehead glistening with sweat. His eyes seemed to watch everything at once.

"Calm down," Marlena said, more than once.

Marlena tried to pull out her datapad at one point but the screen only flickered in the atmospheric electrical instability and she remembered why she couldn't just fly to the site.

After an hour bouncing around the old road, Ethan stopped in front of a small gorge about thirty feet across that ran in both directions as far as they could see.

"Well this is new," he muttered, getting out and inspecting the obstacle.

He walked to the edge of the crevasse, looking down and then following it with his eyes off to the north, squinting against the bright clouds.

"Got any tricks for something like this?" Ethan asked, looking up at Anataur, who only shrugged from the gunner seat atop the AX-15.

"If we have to go around, we may run out of fuel before we get there. I stored some extra fuel near the site for the ride back. But this fissure is something new, it's too deep to try and fill," he said while examining the edge.

"Can we jump it?" Marlena asked, joining him at the edge.

"Not here. If we could find a place where it's narrower and we had some height on our side, then maybe we could do something like that. But we need to pick a direction and keep moving until we find it. There are some dark clouds heading this way," he said, pointing to a darker patch of sky. "North of here is a lake and south is the ravine. Both are pretty dangerous places. I usually stay as far away from them as I can, even when the storm isn't here."

From his higher vantage point Anataur pointed off to the north and said, "Looks like rain coming this way."

Ethan's face went pale as he ushered Marlena back into the AX-15.

"Anataur, you better close the glass dome," Ethan commanded, getting everyone in and driving off quickly to the south.

"Let me guess, the rain is really poisonous flying snakes," Marlena remarked flippantly.

"That would be bad. But, no, it can get pretty acidic and most of the beasts only move in the rains," Ethan explained, driving as fast as he dared along the chasm.

"Will this thing's armor hold against acid?" Anataur asked, worry filling his voice.

"For a while it will, it depends on the storm. I'm more worried about what follows the rains," he replied cryptically.

As they neared the treed ravine, Ethan pointed to a small hill that the chasm had split. It was far narrower here and had a fair bit of height on the nearer side.

"That might work," he said skeptically, driving away from the crack in the ground to line up the jump.

"Might?" Anataur asked, buckling his seatbelt.

Marlena looked from Ethan to the hill and back. Unsure, she looked back passed where Artemis was still asleep in her swinging cot, to where Connor lay quietly.

"It has to," she whispered to no one in particular.

As Ethan was lining up the jump, he had to stomp the brake as a large form leapt from one of the tall trees in the ravine, landing in front of the AX-15. The arachni-bear stood up and roared, parting its dagger-like mandibles, revealing rows of razor teeth beyond. Its many eyes watched the vehicle come to stop some fifty feet away and on eight hairy legs the monstrous thing strafed around, blocking the way to the hill.

"How does it know where we're going?" Marlena cried out.

Her question was lost in the howl of the wind, which slammed into the side of the vehicle, rocking it uncomfortably on the plains.

"That is bigger than I remember. This is bad, I don't think we can outrun it!" Ethan yelled over the wind.

The shouting woke up Artemis, who looked around, startled.

"I'll move it and then you jump the ravine," Anataur sighed reluctantly.

"Don't be-" Artemis began sitting up on her cot.

"Shut up. We're out of time and there is no other way!" Anataur yelled, opening the lid of the gunner pod.

The three inside were objecting as he jumped down from the top of the vehicle. He was no coward and he wasn't wrong, there was no other way. The boy rolled his neck sideways, causing it to crack, and then turned to face the monstrosity blocking their way.

—

The familiar feeling of armor formed around his body and his hands gripped the large hammer as it formed in his hands. He knew he didn't have much time, hearing the ping of a raindrop hit his shoulder followed by the faint hiss. The situation worsened when several more large figures began climbing the trees near the edge of the ravine.

Wasting no time, Anataur roared with all the power his lungs could manage and charged toward the waiting creature, his hammer raised above his head.

The beast tried to sidestep the overhead swing, but Anataur's OMBI-enhanced strength brought the hammer down faster than the arachni-bear had anticipated. The weight of the hit slammed into one of the forelegs on the creature's left side, causing it to howl in pain. Anataur spun in a circle, building momentum, and brought his next swing across at its head.

The arachni-bear managed to duck the blow and swung out with two enormous clawed arms that it had kept hugged around its own body until then. The hit sent Anataur skidding back across the grassy ground, his armor weakened.

More drops of acidic rain began to fall and the arachni-bear held its ground, eying the boy with a thousand tiny eyes.

Beneath his shining black helmet, Pip was smiling despite the dire situation, which was growing more so by the minute. Like many soldiers of Black Squadron, Anataur lived for the challenge of combat.

Howling, he gripped his hammer tightly and charged back in, swinging downward, anticipating the side step left correctly, knowing that the beast's leg was practically crippled. The clawed arms reached up defensively and caught the swing as it came down. The boy looked into the eyes of the creature as he pressed downward with all his strength. The powerful arachni-bear's legs actually began to buckle before it pressed back hard.

Having trained with soldiers like Artemis, Vertigo, and Mephisto, Anataur had many tricks up his sleeve, and as the arachni-bear pressed hard against the hammer, he let it dissipate, leaving its arms up and its abdomen vulnerable. He wasted no movement, charging forward, manifesting a sharp spear with a spike on both ends that he drove through the arachni-bear, moving underneath it as black gore began to pump from the wound. Anataur lifted it on his shoulder and began half carrying, half dragging the beast to the side of the hill.

The crushing weight threatened to overwhelm him as Anataur gritted his teeth, saying, "I will, I will," over and over.

He dragged the dead beast until it was far enough, letting the spear take the weight. He propped the corpse up as he rolled out from beneath it. He kept the spear materialized for a few moments while he sprinted back to the AX-15 before letting it dissipate, letting the dead arachni-bear fall unceremoniously on the ground.

Several more arachni-bears jumped down from the trees in the ravine, and the rain had picked up, causing little wafting lines of smoke to come off the AX-15 and Anataur's armor. A flash of lightning followed by the roar of thunder shook the valley as the broad-shouldered boy got back inside the vehicle, letting his sizzling armor dissipate.

"That was incredible!" Marlena shouted over the storm, nodding as Ethan drove up the hill, accelerating as much as he could, pushing the AX-15's strong engine. They cleared the ravine with a few feet to spare, the roar of thunder following their escape.

Anataur cleaned off the remaining ichor of arachni-bear with the help of Artemis. They looked out the back of the vehicle to see the other arachni-bears retreating back into their ravine, away from the storm.

"They're afraid," Artemis called.

"We aren't safe yet. We aren't going to be able to get away from this storm," Ethan called back. "I'll get us as far as I can but if we have to walk, I'm not sure we'll make it."

"Let me help," Artemis offered, putting her hands on the wall of the AX-15. As she touched the cold interior, she manifested light vehicle armor, which began to absorb the rains.

Tired, Anataur put his hands next to his friend's and reinforced her manifestation.

They drove at the edge of the storm for hours until at last they could see the sea in the distance.

—

Beads of sweat formed upon her forehead as she felt her focus waning. Through her OMBI she could feel every drop of rain sizzle upon the AX-15 armor and every bump in what was left of the road. Her breath came in labored gasps as little dark flecks appeared in her vision.

A strong, familiar hand grasped her shoulder and she felt the weight on her mind ease.

"I got it, Mimi, your turn to rest." Anataur's soothing baritone voice caused her to relax.

She took a breath and let go of the sleek, aerodynamic armor she had been manifesting.

"Wow," Ethan muttered from the driver's seat.

Even in his tense focus, he still seemed awestruck as the armor of his vehicle transformed from slanted sheets into thick, spiked plating.

"Their own personalities affect how they manifest. Even our engineers weren't really sure why," Marlena explained as Ethan just shook his head.

"They are incredible," Ethan offered, turning his attention back to the road.

"Yes, they are. You should see how good Alex is at it, he…" she paused.

Ethan shifted, uncomfortable in his seat.

"Tell me." Ethan glanced over.

"It's just that he is so brave and so confident, Ethan. He

almost single-handedly stopped an invasion force on Aeris, fought off an operative..." she trailed off.

"You and William did a good job with them," Ethan mumbled after a moment.

An orange bolt of lightning struck the ground in front of the AX-15, causing Ethan to curse as he swerved to avoid the rupture it created. The sound of thunder shook the vehicle violently.

The light show behind them, toward the center of the storm, was far more serious. The ground, being struck several hundred times per minute, threw rock and dirt high into the air, ravaging the plains.

Ethan accelerated to stay ahead of the storm, which got a little easier as the ground leveled out.

Artemis climbed into the gunner tube to rest while she watched the storm behind them. In the distance, menacingly tall creatures walked hunched over on two powerful legs, dipping down head first then coming back up swiftly.

"What are those?" she managed.

"I don't know," Ethan replied, eying his mirrors.

Driving near the edge of recklessness, Ethan sped toward the sea, which had finally appeared on the horizon.

"When we get to the ship we are going to need to get inside quickly, this storm is moving fast and I don't want to be caught in the center of it!" she shouted over another boom of thunder.

The plains grew into rolling barren hills, which quickly gave way to the rocky coastline of the Scorpio Sea. Staying up on the cliffs, they drove for several minutes before following a natural descent down to the water. There were more trees near the sea, giving some cover from the rains, which seemed to chase the vehicle deliberately.

They drove along the rocky beach until Ethan turned inland between the break in the treeline; a small camp came into view near the sheer side of a mountain where a shallow tunnel had been cut. The glint of metal inside the cave reflected the light of another lightning strike.

The AX-15 came to a stop in the center of the research camp. From her perch, Artemis could see that the camp had been torn apart. The office trailer was on its side with huge claw marks raked into it and equipment was scattered everywhere.

Ethan grabbed his rifle and brimmed helmet as he exited the vehicle. He walked the perimeter of the base, searching intently, stopping to examine large footprints in the soft ground.

Marlena and Anataur moved through the AX-15, lifting Connor's tube and bringing him outside. They tried to activate its hover capability before Ethan reminded them that it wouldn't work in the electrical storm.

The rain was light but stung a bit as it touched her skin. Despite the pain, Artemis didn't activate her armor.

Marlena's mechanized battle suit seemed to be unaffected by the storm as she lifted one side of the tube. Anataur lifted the other end and they carried it into the small cave, setting it near the sealed door.

Artemis followed Ethan, examining the tracks and the damage to the structure. They crept inside, through a broken window, the smell of old blood still lingering in the air.

She pointed out a blood splatter on one wall and grimaced apologetically to Ethan, whose forehead furrowed with worry.

"There," she said, pointing at an overturned table.

A small, leather-bound book was pressed between the table and what had been the ceiling of the modular office. Ethan picked it up, examining it quickly, and put it in the pocket of his coat.

"What is it?" Artemis asked.

"Dr. Arminus' journal. He was here," he explained as they walked out of the shredded building.

"Wouldn't a datapad be more practical?" she asked, walking after him.

"Maybe above the storm, but down here electronics don't work right, remember?" Ethan reminded her absently.

Artemis and Ethan joined the other two at the cave as the rains began to pick up.

"It looks like several razor fish attacked during the last storm. Someone was inside when they tore it apart," He pointed back at the modular, "and my fuel reserves are missing."

"How close to Tiberius Falls can we get without a refill?" Marlena asked, looking up sharply from Connor's tube.

Ethan leaned against the side of the cave. "Not far. If we can get out between storms, there is a small chance we could cross the distance on foot. But, this may have been a one way trip."

"Does the tide come up this far?" Artemis gulped, nodding toward the modular.

Ethan stared back at her quizzically for a moment before shaking his head. "Oh, no. Razor fish live underwater most of the time, but during storms they hunt some of the other beasts on land. They walk on four legs and look more like jackal than a fish."

"This place is one nightmare after another," she mumbled, sitting back against the rocks.

"Let's get that door open. The storm is picking up and it won't be long before this area is infested by those nightmares." Ethan pointed at the door.

Ethan loaded his rifle and stood at the mouth of the cave, his watchful eyes scanning from shore to tree line. Anataur and Artemis moved to the door, and began inspecting it.

A shriek from outside caused them to look back. The noise was quickly followed by a second and third scream. Ethan backed into the cave slowly.

"Screamers! We need to hurry. They have our scent by now. They are blind, but they hunt by smell and navigate by sound," Ethan whispered frantically.

Artemis turned back to the door, feeling along its seam with her fingertips. She reached through her OMBI to the door, asking it to open.

There was no response.

"Anataur, you try," she whispered, manifesting her bow.

She scampered to the mouth of the cave without a sound. She stood opposite Ethan, manifesting an arrow.

Anataur had his eyes closed, with his hands on the door.

"I can feel the power cables in the walls," he stated to the others, "and something deeper, like eyes watching me inside. But they scatter when I get close."

Beads of sweat formed upon his brow as he shut his eyes tighter.

"Hurry, Pip," Artemis whispered, looking back at him.

The boy turned and shrugged.

"I tried everything I could to command it to open and nothing," he whispered.

"Great," Ethan said under his breath.

Another shriek echoed from outside, this one much closer.

"Could there be another entrance open somewhere?" Marlena asked, looking from Anataur to Artemis.

"Maybe, the OMBIcademy had an entrance like this plus a few cargo and docking bays that we used, although, we didn't go into most parts of it," the boy remarked, staring intently at the door.

Artemis watched as a pale-skinned creature appeared at the edge of the tree line, sniffing the air. It was humanoid but completely devoid of hair, walking slightly hunched over. Its large hands stretched out, revealing jagged claws as it sniffed for several seconds. Everyone in the cave sat very still, hardly breathing. After a moment, it tilted its bulbous head toward the cave and opened its mouth to reveal a row of long, pointed teeth.

The scream it emitted caused chills to run down Artemis' spine.

"Anataur, move Connor's tube to the back of the cave," Marlena ordered, drawing her pistol.

She joined Artemis and Ethan at the cave's entrance.

The scream was answered by hundreds more, which echoed so loud, Artemis could barely hear the crack of thunder directly above them. Under the now pouring rain, the hunched, pale screamers charged toward the cave.

—

Artemis shot first and second as her arrows bit into the foreheads of the first two screamers to emerge. She continued the steady barrage which, for a moment, seemed to hold back the wave of monsters. Lightning flashed causing her to blink and, in the span of a moment, the ground between the cave and the trees was swarming with the hunched monstrosities. The creatures leap onto the AX-15 and off it toward the cave. Some fell upon their clawed arms, using all four limbs to carry them even more swiftly.

Ethan fired his rifle and reloaded with expert speed, his prac-ticed aim blasting through the lead screamers and into the ones behind.

Marlena held her shots until one got close and she took it down with a controlled pair of bullets to the chest as it reared up.

Artemis, true to her namesake, did the most damage as she fired a steady stream of arrows. One burst into a heavy net im-mediately in front of them just as she fired it. Its anchors bit hard into the cave's walls, giving them a small barrier against the nimble screamers. The ones that got close got tangled long enough for Marlena to dispatch them with her pistol. Artemis' next arrows erupted into small explosions, engulfing groups of screamers in fire and knocking others onto the ground, disrupt-ing their momentum.

In her mind Marlena figured that the choke point was good

for defense, already nearly thirty of the ugly creatures were dead and many more were wounded. She knew that they couldn't keep it up forever though, she and Ethan would eventually run out of ammo and without their support, even with Artemis' unlimited supply of arrows, they would be overrun.

In the chaos she thought she heard someone calling her name, but dismissed it until Anataur pulled her shoulder back and pointing. The dark metal door was open with Connor's tube just inside.

"Fall back!" she ordered, rushing to the back of the cave.

With Anataur's help, she pulled Connor's tube deeper into the structure.

The twang of the bow string never slowed, punctuated by rifle shots and shrieks of pain from outside.

Ethan crossed inside, loading another round. Artemis followed quickly behind him, walking backward and continuing her barrage.

"Why isn't the door closing?" Ethan barked.

Anataur just shrugged.

Artemis and Ethan used the narrow cave entrance and net well. They had nearly created a wall of pale bodies when a large hand tore the netting and bodies away, followed by a huge, tusked snout, which poked into the cave. The tusked creature was nearly too big for the entrance, but pushed in anyway, clawing its way forward and causing the entire ground to shake.

Ethan and Artemis continued shooting but it didn't slow, forcing its way through the cavern. Artemis quickly improvised, firing an arrow into the stone ceiling of the cavern just outside the door. The explosion destroyed the rocky cave, causing the mountain above to rumble downward, blocking the door, filling the corridor with a cloud of dust.

Darkness followed the collapse and eventually the rumbling ceased.

They took a few minutes to catch their breath, coughing the dust from their lungs. After a bit, their hearing returned to normal and they could hear the distant sound of dripping. The hall, faintly illuminated by OMBI light, cast long shadows in the foreboding halls.

"How will we get out?" Marlena whispered.

Anataur shrugged. "Explosives, hammering, digging, it's not that far."

"It's not far enough," Ethan corrected. "That pig-faced thing is one of the most dedicated hunters on Dytopa II. We call them reapers. It has our scent and it won't give up on us until it has us. Once it gets itself unstuck, it'll dig until it gets to this door. It might be wounded, we hit it hard, but we can't forget about it. Worse, those screamers will be helping it."

The four of them sat quietly for nearly a minute, digesting the man's words.

"I guess," Marlena said after a few moments, "we don't have to worry about digging our way out of here."

Picking up one end of Connor's tube, she motioned for Anataur to grab the other. He hesitated slightly but did as instructed. Artemis led the group, her eyes enhanced by her OMBI.

Ethan took the rear, looking back often as the sound of shifting rock and creaking of the old ship kept him on edge.

"How did you open the door?" Artemis asked Anataur, pausing in the dark hallway.

"I didn't," Anataur said quietly. "I think it was Mephisto's brother."

Marlena and Ethan exchanged a troubled glance.

"All right then," Artemis answered, peering into the darkness. "Here we go."

CHAPTER 8

A maze of memories

H E BLINKED AWAY THE SLEEP IN HIS EYES, FIGHTING
against the induced exhaustion. The sedatives were
wearing off but Alex sat still in the small cell, the force
field humming quietly in the cold, gray room.

His eyes were closed, focusing on his OMBI, listening. He
could hear communications faintly from around the station still,
although he couldn't make out what they were saying. They
sounded like a distant conversation on the other side of a wall,
which he knew was his 3rd inhibitor. Forcing his consciousness
deeper, he felt the ship groaning against the pressure, fighting
against the vacuum of space.

He tried listening for Skoll, but it was too difficult to sort
through the noise around him.

As his consciousness careened through the electronics on
the ship, he could feel the dark spots. He somehow knew that
they were the 4th inhibitors from other OMBIs. There were two,
one was heading his way and the other was a bit farther off. It
hadn't been there earlier, but it was definitely there now. It even
felt familiar to him somehow.

When Vertigo arrived at his cell with an armed escort, Alex
had expected them. He feigned a stumble as he stood up and

accepted the plastic restraints they put on his wrists without resisting.

"I guess he inhaled quite a bit of that gas," a guard commented.

Alex let the soldiers lead him down the halls and into a lift. Vertigo eyed him dubiously out of the corner of his eye as Alex kept up his ruse. He forced his mind into a haze, blinking several times, letting exhaustion find his eyes.

The lift stopped a few levels above the detention area and Alex found himself on the medical deck. He could feel several 311 AFMR around him and one that seemed to be waiting for him at the end of the hallway. They cut his restraints and strapped him to a chair facing a mirrored wall in the operating room.

"What's going on?" he sputtered quietly.

"They are going to remove your OMBI, Alex. Harruhama thinks that without it, Skoll will accept a new pilot," Vertigo explained sympathetically.

They had been at odds, but the two had once been friends and both of them understood that the removal of an OMBI was likely to kill the host.

"He wants to kill me, Austin?" Alex mumbled, letting his head fall down heavily.

"They told me that you could survive if we remove it right," Vertigo replied as the AFMR began to lay out operating tools.

"This is..." Alex began coughing, "the Nostus?"

"Yeah, how did you know?" Vertigo said, while watching the AFMR began spinning a small saw.

"I didn't," Alex smiled, fully lucid.

Through his OMBI Alex focused on the saw. The blade split the restraint and quickly slashed across, splitting the other.

"What the...?" Vertigo barked, falling back.

"As if Vector could bond with Skoll!" Alex laughed, hopping to his feet.

"How did you know it was going to be me?" Vector called out from the other side of the observation glass.

Smiling, Alex shut his eyes briefly, summoning his strength through his OMBI, letting the familiar twin blades manifest into his waiting hands.

His eyes still shut, Alex deftly blocked Austin's sword as it swung toward his throat. He felt where the sword was faster than his eyes could have seen it and he deftly deflected another strike. He could feel the other OMBI coming around from the observation room.

His eyes popped open, glowing a fierce shade of green as he launched into a series of cunning swipes, high and low with his twin blades.

Vertigo fell back, desperately blocking the attacks like a kid trying to swat away a typhoon. He had almost lost the fight entirely when Vector burst into the room, his armor already manifested and a short spear in one hand.

Vector charged at Alex, who hadn't raised his own armor. Alex quickly deflected the attack, using Vector's momentum to maneuver the boy into the glass of the observation room.

Vector hit the wall hard, causing the glass to shatter into the room beyond, revealing a pair of observers. One was a tall man in a lab coat, furiously taking notes. The other was General Harruhama.

"There you are." Alex grinned, pointing one blade at the old man as he deflected Vertigo's attack with the other.

Alex looked straight into the man's surprised eyes. His scimitar swung over his shoulder, behind his back, picking off Vector's short spear.

"Stop him!" the general commanded, moving to the back wall of the room, his eyes wide.

"As if," Alex laughed, spinning a full circle, knocking away sword and spear.

Alex's smile didn't diminish as the 311 AFMR grabbed Vertigo from behind, hindering him long enough for Alex to turn his full fury toward Vector. The two had fought in practice before, but Alex came on moving faster than Vector had ever seen anyone move.

"Crap, help!" he yelled as Alex's swords worked his spear up high before dissipating.

Alex grabbed Vector's right arm and pulled it behind his back easily, forcing the bigger boy to let his spear dissipate. Alex quickly tapped the other boy's OMBI, expertly navigating its menus. Alex forced Vector's armor to dissipate and slugged him hard in the back of the head, sending him sprawling into the operating chair, unconscious.

Vertigo was just getting untangled with the AFMR when Alex was upon him, launching a series of rapid strikes with his fists, knocking the wind out of Vertigo's lungs and punching him hard in the face.

Alex turned back toward the observation room, finding it empty. A moment later an alarm blared.

"All available troops to get to the medical deck and subdue the prisoner," a voice commanded through the speakers.

Taking a deep breath, he calmed himself long enough to order the AFMR to remove Austin's 4th inhibitor. As an afterthought, he issued an order to sedate and remove Vector's inhibitor too.

Focusing, Alex ran in a blur of motion into the hall and toward a ventilation duct. With a powerful jump, he burst through the grate, landing nimbly upon his hands and knees.

Crawling with enhanced speed, he quickly made his way off the medical deck, heading deeper into the ship. When he got near what he thought was the bow of the Nostus, he manifested a steel-like coating around his hands with his OMBI fist weapon, tearing holes in the duct as he climbed upward.

Alex moved so fast that he arrived at the bridge ahead of Harruhama. He dropped into the room, quickly disabling the navigator and communications officer with a surprise attack. Looking through the reinforced bay windows, he could see Earth's moon spinning quietly in the darkness.

Wasting no time, he placed his hand on the console at the helm of the ship, accessing the central core. His OMBI interfaced with the Nostus in seconds as he systematically disabled and locked out control of the escape pods. He kept the docking bay that Skoll was in active, as he then disabled the other four fighter bays.

Thinking quickly, Alex set navigation controls on a course for Earth, entering the only coordinates he had in his OMBI, the *Return* function's directions to the Black Army barracks in the OMBIcademy. He managed to alter the course slightly so that the ship wouldn't land directly on the OMBIcademy before disconnecting.

Turning back to the communication's station, he sent an encoded message to William's datapad.

To: William Mercer

Subject: Harruhama's going down, bring reinforcements.

Message: 25°56′56.5″N, 131°18′54.0″E

Sent.

Alex then left the bridge through the same ventilation duct he had ascended, barely slowing his descent until he got to the level of the cargo bay that held Skoll.

Alex burst through the grate into a surprised-looking man in a plain uniform, knocking him to the ground as Alex rolled through the fall and came up on his feet.

"Oh! Please help me up?" the man asked meekly.

"Sorry!" Alex said, moving to help the man.

As Alex reached toward him, twin blades manifested in the boy's waiting hands. He swung downward, straight toward the man's neck.

The operative cursed as he sprung away from the prone position, a thin blade appearing in his left hand.

The man came at Alex in a flash, his thin blade deflected by a waiting scimitar. Several small darts shot forward from the man's right hand, which bounced harmlessly off Alex's armor as it manifested around his body.

His attack defeated, the operative danced back several quick steps, producing a compact assault pistol from under his coat. The barrage of bullets ricocheted off Alex's shield as Alex copied the weapon and manifested it in his hand as one of his curved swords dissipated.

Alex's bullets hit the dodging target, who smartly covered his exposed face, letting his battle armor absorb the impact.

The two stood facing off, the operative nodding respectfully to the resourceful boy.

"How did you know?" Operative two hissed.

"I fought an operative before." Alex shrugged. "My mom killed one, my stepdad killed another, I guess it's my turn."

The operative frowned as he eyed the boy. He nodded carefully and in one swift motion, turned and ran in the opposite direction.

Alex didn't pursue, but instead walked forward into the cargo bay. He cut the heavy straps holding Skoll down and boarded, settling in for the ride. He didn't exit the Nostus, knowing the orbital defenses of Earth would be difficult to navigate from the outside, so he elected to ride the frigate down. It was a long ride from the Moon to the OMBIcademy, so Alex sat back, getting comfortable in his battle suit.

—

On Earth, William was in mid-flight in an SLX-Condor on his way toward Japan with a group of rebellion leaders when he got the message from Alex. He wasn't close, but he was glad he was heading in the right direction as he gave orders for reinforcements to meet him there. They had been on their way to Harruhama's personal residence in Tokyo to look for clues on his whereabouts when the mission was abruptly cancelled.

William relayed the message to the other leaders who began to issue orders for free men troops in the area to get to Kita-Daito.

"Hurry," was all William told the pilot, feeling that the end of his long road was near.

—

The rumble of rock faded behind them as they crept down the dark hall that gently curved out of sight. The ground was covered with a thick layer of dust, which appeared to have never been disturbed before now. They passed by intersecting corridors, but always chose to move straight ahead.

"This isn't like anywhere I have been on the OMBIcademy," Artemis said suddenly.

They paused by a set of doors, neither of which opened. They tried moving Connor's tube near them, but nothing happened. During the break, Ethan fished Arminus' journal out of his pocket and flipped through the pages. Using the light of Artemis' OMBI, Ethan read out loud.

"August 18th, 2121: I am leaving Tiberius Falls today. Since our last visit to the object, I have been unable to sleep. I feel as though there is something there, calling me. The storms won't stop for several more months, but I cannot wait. I won't be taking my escort along, it would be unfair of me to risk his life."

"This isn't like Miles. He was always the cautious one. Eccentric, but cautious," Ethan frowned.

"Did something different happen the last time you two were here? Could he have found something he didn't tell you about?" Marlena asked, leaning against Connor's tube.

Ethan only shrugged and turned the pages of the journal, looking for the answer.

"August 21st, 2121: I have traversed the cloud-lands without incident. My fear is that Ethan may risk himself coming after me, so I blocked the road. It wasn't easy, but I got lucky with a break in the clouds. The cutting attracted a mist wolf pack, but I was gone before they arrived. I drove through the night staying behind a herd of giant bipedal beasts that seemed to ignore my AX-11. They were following a storm that I had managed to stay out of. I reached the base camp ahead of another storm, but I cannot sleep. I hear the voice in my head louder here. I will wait for the light of day and seek a way into, ship. Ship? Is that what this is?"

They sat very quietly in the hallway, all feeling uneasy.

"Could there have been another entrance?" Ethan asked to himself. "This dust hasn't been disturbed, so we know he didn't get in here."

"I have heard stories," Anataur began, "of the early days after the discovery of the OMBI. When they were uninhibited, the electronics would communicate back with the operator. Could he have found one? Could that explain the voices?"

"We rode back together after the last expedition. I didn't notice anything like this on him," Ethan said, tapping Artemis' OMBI.

"Is there any more?" Marlena asked impatiently.

Ethan continued reading the hastily written last page of the journal.

"August 21st 2121: I have found it! There is another entrance on the far side of the mountain. It may have been some kind of cargo port. It is a wide opening, but that level of the ship has been infested with beasts that have made their nests inside. The rains have picked up and the reapers are out. I killed a small razor fish and will cover my scent with its pheromone gland. I am coming…"

The page ended with a smear of blood.

Marlena felt the blood drain from her face.

"That sounds bad," she whispered. "We better get going."

"Are you sure? We could be walking into a nightmare," Ethan commented, putting the journal away.

"We don't have a choice, we may be caught between two nightmares. But forward is the only direction we can go," Marlena resolved, "I'll carry Connor from here. Anataur, I want you free to fight if we run into anything big."

Anataur nodded as he opened Connor's tube. As it opened, the hallway was suddenly flooded with light. They all shut their eyes against the unexpected brightness before the lights flickered and died.

Swallowing her fear, the raven-haired woman picked up her son, easily carrying his weight, her strength enhanced by the strange operative battle armor.

"Let's go," she said, walking down the hallway.

Artemis moved quickly, taking the lead again with her best friend by her side. Ethan took a deep breath and, after a moment, followed the determined group.

A short time later the group slowed, noticing a dim light emanating from a side corridor. Artemis moved forward quietly, peering around the corner and tilting her head curiously. She waved the others forward as she studied the hall.

Around the corner the hall ended in an open doorway, dim moonlight coming through into the corridor. Artemis moved through, looking around the grassy hillside. The others followed her through onto the strange hill.

"This isn't Dytopa," Ethan remarked, examining the ground.

"No, it isn't," a little boy's voice said from behind them.

The kid stood in front of the now closed doorway. His blue eyes were dark in the moonlight and his mop of brown hair tossed about in the cool breeze. Marlena recognized the boy.

"William?" she whispered breathlessly.

"No, I am the Training Optimization Program Omega," the boy replied, "or, what's left of him."

"What do you mean, 'what's left'?" Marlena asked, laying Connor gently on the grass and walking over to study the boy.

"I was killed on August 7th, 2121 during a battle in the Sol system. What you see is what remains of me in the memory of my initiator," Omega explained impassively.

"August seventh … You are Connor's OMBI AI, aren't you?" Marlena asked.

"Yes and no. I am the memory of the manifestation of the initiator's OMBI AI," the boy said, unblinking.

"Then how are you here?" Artemis asked, looking from the boy to Connor.

Omega smiled. His image faded slightly and took on the appearance of Connor as a four-year-old boy, wearing the clothes he had on the last time Marlena had seen him before going on her final mission for the UEDF.

"Isn't heaven where we go when we die? Isn't that why you're here, Mommy?" the image of Connor asked.

"That's right, baby," she sniffled, tears forming in her eyes as she moved to hug the boy in front of her. She stopped short as the image flickered and turned back into the boyish form of William Mercer.

"How can we help, Connor?" Marlena asked, wiping the tear from her cheek. "How can we help you both?"

Omega pointed behind them. They all turned to see a house that hadn't been there before, a short distance away.

"What are we supposed…?" Marlena began, turning back to see an empty hillside and a closed metallic door standing strangely upon it.

She took a deep breath and turned back toward the house. Picking up Connor, she walked forward with determined strides. The other three followed silently.

The house stood tall above them. Though she hadn't seen it in six years, Marlena recognized it as the house that she, William, and the kids had built together. It was far larger than Marlena remembered it, like she was seeing it from the eyes of a four-year-old kid. Inside she heard an unmistakable cry of anguish.

She ran inside, bursting through the door to see William Mercer on his knees, holding a slip of paper on his hand. A ten-year-old Alex stood beside him, his fist clenched with rage. Connor stood frozen, eyes wide, while holding a toy spaceship at the top of the stairs.

"What happened, William?" Connor asked innocently, walking carefully down the stairs, clutching the banister.

William was sobbing, his tears falling freely from his blue eyes.

"Alex? What happened?" Connor pleaded urgently.

Alex looked at Connor. The rage in his eyes reminded Marlena of a wild fire as he stormed off past his younger brother, running upstairs and slamming a far-off door. Connor walked slowly up to William, his worried eyes looking from the man to the paper on the ground.

"Are you okay?" Connor asked, trying to look at William's face.

Connor picked up the paper and started reading out loud, sounding out the words carefully.

Looking over his shoulder, Marlena, still carrying her unconscious son, read the note as well. "We regret to inform you that your wife, Captain Marlena Mercer, Phoenix: KIA on a mission in the Eagle Nebula on..." She stopped as Connor asked William what "KIA" meant.

William's voice was barely a whisper as he spoke, "She's dead, Connor. I am so sorry."

The tears in Connor's eyes broke Marlena's heart. His image ran right through her, running upstairs screaming. She ran after the ghostly image, still carrying Connor's ten-year-old comatose body. She ran through the door to his bedroom, exiting out into a hallway in a different part of the ship. The others followed quickly.

They paused in the hallway, giving Marlena a minute to collect herself.

Ethan cast his eyes to the floor, taking deep breathes to steady himself. Seeing his children in so much pain unnerved the man more than he would admit. He didn't know William but, after the scene in the training room, he felt incredibly sympathetic for him.

"I'm sorry, Marlena," he whispered, "I'm sorry, Alex and Connor."

After several minutes, Marlena got up and began walking down the hallway. Artemis stopped them as they reached the crossing hallway, pointing out the dust in the main corridor that had been completely removed.

They couldn't discern any tracks in the area and, listening, they couldn't hear anything moving nearby.

"Which way do we go?" Anataur asked.

"Which way, Connor?" Marlena whispered to her unconscious son.

A light down the main hallway flickered and Marlena nodded in its direction. The smell of this level of the ship was not the stale dusty smell of the level they had entered on, but a slight breeze brought a damp, musky scent. Walking slowly, Ethan removed his rifle and held it tightly.

A strange, high-pitched call pierced the silence that sounded like some kind of bird. They all looked at Ethan, who only shrugged. They passed by a doorway that was open and, looking inside, saw a series of strange large pods that ran from the ceiling to the floor. Most of them had been cracked open, the insides completely empty other than dark stains. Only one tube stood undamaged and it had clearly been opened recently.

They searched the room but, finding nothing else, continued down the hall. A short distance from the pod room, the walls of the hallway were stained with increasingly frequent dark splatters that caused shivers to run down Marlena's spine.

"Are you sure, Connor?" she asked her boy quietly, getting no response.

"It looks like something bad happened here," Anataur groaned, inspecting the walls.

"It looks like it happened a long time ago though," Ethan added, decreasing the tension.

A light flicked ahead. When they got to it they found the remains of what appeared to be an elevator shaft. They could see a light far below, which caused Marlena to wonder just how big the ship was. Looking up, she could see a few floors above, but the doors were all shut.

"Let me take him," Anataur said to Marlena, gently taking Connor in his strong arms and hoisting him over his shoulder.

He held Connor with one arm and manifested a fist weapon with the other as he sat down at the edge of the shaft and spun, grabbing the edge with his hand.

"There's a ladder on the near wall," he said, climbing over to it while keeping Connor steady.

The group made their way downward, deeper into the wrecked ship. Strange sounds emanated from the various levels that were sealed off by closed doors. The light source was closer than it had appeared from above, coming through a door that was only slightly ajar.

It was not the bottom floor, but Anataur managed to keep hold of Connor and the ladder while he formed a sickle in his right hand. He used the weapon to hook the open door and pulled hard. The door didn't budge at first, but Artemis did the same thing above Anataur and the two of them got it open enough for the group to squeeze through.

Jumping into the opening, Artemis went first, disappearing for a moment then returning, reaching out her hand. Anataur shifted Connor to his other shoulder and leaned out far enough for Artemis to grab him.

Anataur took the boy back when he climbed through and the two waited for Marlena and Ethan, helping them through. The area appeared to be a catwalk to a hanger that had obviously seen battle. The sidewall was completely torn away and a huge pile of rocks seemed to have slid into the room below them.

"This must have been where they hit. I wonder what made them crash?" Artemis asked, looking at Marlena.

"You're probably right, that doesn't look like any kind of damage I've seen from a weapon," Marlena replied, examining the wall.

They walked across the catwalk that led to an open doorway and into a hall beyond, where they heard a strange rapid clicking noise. Ethan shushed the others and moved to the front of the group. Marlena took Connor back from Anataur, hoisting him up in her arms.

The clicking, as it turned out, came from the mandibles of several arachni-bears that were down the hallway to the left. Ethan put his finger to his mouth and crept into the hallway to the right, motioning for the others to follow. The clicking faded behind them and they walked through another long, rounded hallway. A breeze from a side hall to the left led them into a dark room, which lit up when they all had entered. It appeared to be the observation deck of the OMBIcademy.

Major Sanders was standing next to Connor near a dark window, looking down on a battle that none of them could see.

"Listen, kid, I didn't invite you up here to listen to you complain about how unfair your life is. I brought you up here because I had something important to tell you," Sanders said sternly, causing Connor to look at him sharply. The look of defiance burned in his eyes.

"Well, what is it?" Connor stamped impatiently.

"It's about your stepfather. Three months ago, during a routine investigation, William Mercer along with twenty members of a special operations team died in an explosion at your home in Healdsburg."

There was a long silence between the two, Marlena could see Connor's face redden at the news, and the other three members of the team put their heads down and turned away.

The image of Connor burst into tears.

"An explosion that killed twenty-one people during a routine investigation?!" Connor screamed, tears pouring down his cheeks.

"Yeah, kid, that's what the report said," Sanders mumbled.

"That is a load of crap! What kind of investigation involves twenty spec-ops soldiers?! They went there to kill him because he hated the EMC! Only he must have killed them too! You bastards took my mom, my brother, and now William!" Connor screamed hysterically.

"I have nobody!" Connor fell to his knees, sobbing heavily.

"Untrue," Omega said, appearing next to Connor, looking down at him sympathetically. The image shifted, leaving the room looking different, unadorned and old. The other Connor and Major Sanders were gone, but Omega stared at where they had been.

"It was the third parent he lost in his short life, and we

couldn't find Alex either," Omega said, turning and looking at Marlena. There was sadness in the hologram's eyes.

"William and Connor were close?" Ethan asked.

"They were best friends for his whole life. William was always there for him, always patient with him, always had an answer for him, and even after the EMC took him he still had William, until that day," Omega explained in a sorrowful tone. "He still dreams about it, even now."

"But William is alive, he faked his death," Marlena said to Omega.

"He is alive, my sweet boy, and we're going to find him," she said again to Connor's unconscious body.

"That is good news, we will be glad." Omega smiled. "We are almost there. You must be brave, the next place is very scary."

Omega's face frowned, his brow furrowing with concern as he faded away. The door on the far side of the room opened slowly and they walked through into what looked like the anteroom of the OMBIcademy's observation lounge.

The room appeared to have power, lit by the few unbroken lights in the ceiling. It was a welcome change from the dim illumination of OMBI light. A scream from the double door to the left caused them all to stop and produce weapons. Rifle, bow, and hammer came up as the group moved to the doorway, opening it slowly.

The room beyond was clearly an observation deck of some kind, poorly lit in the center, with strange large blocks scattered throughout. There were five large windows, all of which were broken. The screaming echoed again from one of the windows on the left. They crept to the edge, looking down onto a holographic battlefield, full of beasts that howled as the landscape changes rippled throughout.

Trees faded to desert, which slowly grew into dunes, then to hills, the sand falling away to reveal grass underneath. The screamers tried to remain in the trees and, as the landscapes changed, they howled and ran. Arachni-bears kept trying to climb the trees or would rush to newly formed ravines as a pig-faced, bipedal reaper slammed itself against a red door on the opposite side of the arena.

The other four arenas were all in various states of destruction. One was flooded and the corpses of several strange, long-legged, white furry creatures floated in the water. Another was malfunctioning, creating walls that fell to the floor, slamming into the gory remains of multiple beasts that had found their way in. The final two rooms were dark, without the light of the artificial sun. The howling and wailing in them sent shivers down Marlena's spine.

Ethan nodded forward to a glass door that led into a circular elevator. They quickly entered, feeling the lift lowering them deeper into the ship. At the bottom the tube opened into a large, circular room with a platform in the middle.

In the center of the platform, a bulbous, yellow head stretched up into the air nearly twenty feet high, with one large eye that watched the group as they approach. The thing had six long tentacles, four of which were held in metal shackles, connected to the walls by large chains. Two were hanging from chains, but were no longer attached to the creature's body. The area where they had been ripped away on the creature looked bad; black gore dried up where it had spilled ages before.

"She's beautiful, isn't she?" a man cried out from the top of the platform.

"Dr. Arminus?" Ethan asked, barely recognizing the man.

His hair had gone stark white and stood on end. The man's arms were covered in black gore up to the shoulder and his eyes were bloodshot with dark bags underneath them.

"Ah, Ethan, good! It's good that you're here to see this. You brought friends to see too. Fine, fine," the doctor rambled, as the group approached.

Spotting the two OMBI soldiers, the bulbous yellow creature let out a piercing cry.

"Stay away! You must keep away! She doesn't like those!" he yelled, pointing at the wrists of Anataur and Artemis.

The two exchanged a worried glance and stopped on the stairway. Marlena and Ethan stopped as well, unsure what to make of the macabre scene.

"What are you doing, Doctor?" Ethan asked as the man ran around, looking at the ground as if he lost something.

"She contacted me, Ethan! She told me that I could live forever and rule Dytopa if I helped her! She is an angel, don't you see?" the man yelled, falling to his knees.

"Where are the OMBI, uh, the bracers kept?" Marlena asked, trying to get the doctor's attention.

"I threw them out! She told me that I couldn't use them. I tossed them through the windows upstairs!" he mimicked the throw.

"Well that's great," Marlena muttered, looking back at Anataur and Artemis, who were both visibly tense at the idea of going into any of those rooms.

"This is sick! This thing is clearly a prisoner!" Ethan yelled, trying to reason with his one-time partner.

"Right! It looks that way, but, I assure you that the Xudoks were enslaved by the sinister Cryptoliths! We need to free her! FREE HER!" Arminus screamed.

"He's right," Ethan said suddenly, laying his rifle down.

It started as a subtle whisper in the back of her mind and formed into a thought, *the Xudoks need to be free.* The only way they'll share immortality was to free them, after all.

"Nope!" Anataur yelled, his OMBI forming a large hammer in his hands.

He charged forward, knocking Dr. Arminus aside, and slammed his hammer down hard on the eye of the bulbous yellow creature. Several arrows flew over Anataur's shoulder, biting the soft flesh of the creature as Artemis moved to back up her friend.

The suggestion faded from Marlena's mind and she shook away the thought before it really took hold. The thing had tried to control her thoughts, leaving her feeling incredibly violated and somehow sticky.

"Nope, nope, nope," Anataur continued as he swung his hammer over and over into the giant beast, which recoiled and let out a series of screams.

The attack continued until Dr. Arminus dashed into Anataur, knocking him off the platform. The man stood up and charged down the stairway at Artemis. A shot rang out from Ethan's large rifle, striking Arminus in the chest, knocking him backwards. The man did not go down, however, and reared up, laughing.

"Good shot! Good shot! I knew I hired you for a reason! Won't work though!" he shouted hysterically, pulling his coat aside to reveal mechanized battle armor. "Found this in a tube upstairs! Makes me strong! So so strong!"

"There is only one weakness!" Marlena yelled back, causing Arminus to pause and stare at her.

She drew her sidearm with her free arm and, in one fluid motion, pulled the trigger, aiming for Arminus' head. The man went down in a slump, causing the creature to bellow loudly, thrashing against its restrains. Artemis' arrow took it in the eye, detonating. The blast left a smoking hole where the eye had been as black ichor seeped from the wound. The Xudok continued to scream and Artemis fired two more explosive arrows into it before it collapsed.

Anataur, in a daze, walked around the platform back to the stairs, where he was greeted by Artemis.

"Nice work, Pip! But how did you stop it from controlling you? I felt my OMBI trying to help me, but I couldn't really hear what it was saying," Artemis asked, breathing hard.

"Yeah, it got in quick, how did you resist it?" Marlena asked, moving between them.

Anataur's face went pale as he shrugged. "That thing made me feel all sticky. I hate being sticky."

CHAPTER 9

The Pawn

"**W**E'RE GOING DOWN!" HARRUHAMA shouted through his communicator in the secondary control room.

"You have lost Earth and have not eliminated any of the targets. You are not worthy of His power," Daniel Asher growled back.

"There is still hope! Once we land, I can get inside the OMBIcademy and seal it up. We are on the brink of taking back the colonies," Harruhama said, frantically waving his hands.

"Already, allies of the one boy you could not defeat are landing around the OMBIcademy; you have lost. You may as well retain your honor and take your own life," Asher said.

The idea of seppuku made the blood drain from Hurruhama's face. He ended the transmission without another word. He was not a coward, but he had long ago given up on the idea that he would ever die after he decoded the signal from deep in the Pacific Ocean. For thirty-five years, the man had done everything that he was told to do; he had taken on the role of a global dictator and now that he was getting old, he was not about to let go of the immortality he was promised.

⁓

Alone in the cargo hold, Alex waited longer than he expected. The ship wasn't moving incredibly fast, but soon the curvature of the Earth came into view and Alex watched it while monitoring his motion sensor. There was some, as soldiers and engineers ran through the halls trying to stop the ship. They didn't spend much time trying to sort through the code that Alex installed to lock the ship's controls; most dashed frantically around, seeming to go between their stations and the escape pods and back. At one point during the three-hour flight, a group of soldiers entered the cargo bay, but when Skoll turned its draconic head, they retreated.

There was nothing they could do except go down. Alex's approach was good, having brought many frigates down through atmosphere on Aeris VII. It wasn't long before the landing thrusters were firing and the ship laid itself gently down in a surprisingly smooth landing, partly in the ocean and part on the island.

Alex didn't waste any time, bursting forth from the cargo hold in Skoll, flying up and surveying the scene around him.

"There you are, nice work!" William's voice congratulated over the com.

"Oh, hey, William! Where are you?" Alex asked.

"At your eleven o'clock. We landed on the OMBIcademy platform. Major Sanders let some of our troops in to secure the facility. They are keeping the students in their barracks and detaining the guards. Colonel Setzer locked himself in his office though and disabled the lift. That guy is a loon!" William chuckled slightly.

"What do you mean?" Alex shared the laugh.

"Alex, watch out!" came the unexpected reply.

From the shallow waves below Skoll, the form of a great

serpent burst forth, spraying water high into the air as it tried to wrap around Skoll's legs.

Alex was moving as William spoke, flying higher into the air, avoiding the cunning attack. Skoll's curved scimitars manifested in its strong metal hands and Alex dove back downward at his foe. The serpent ship dodged away in a swirling pattern, only taking a few minor scratches, which did little damage against its strong, flexible hull.

"Not bad, boy, but Jörmungandr doesn't fall so easily!" the familiar voice taunted over the com as the ship swirled toward Skoll, its jaws snapping menacingly.

Alex managed to dodge the strike by dropping low near the water and raising his blades above his head. As fast as he was, Alex's counter attack missed the swerving enemy, which flew off in a mesmerizing pattern, quickly circling him.

—

Below the battle of the dragon knight and the serpent, fighting had broken out between the soldiers escaping from the Nostus and the free men on the ground. The free men had fortified the area and were holding the ground well against the pressing attack, keeping the enemy soldiers pinned on the rocky beach.

William, wearing his mechanized battle suit, duster, and wide-brimmed cowboy hat, watched from the landing pad of the OMBIcademy as the fighting moved onto the shoreline of the island. By chance, out of the corner of his eye, William saw the flash of light, the reflection of a metal object on the beach headed the other way, around their position toward the OMBIcademy.

Leaving the fighting to the free men commanders, William ran back with his enhanced speed, toward the OMBIcademy cutting off the fleeing group, jumping down into the rocks in front of them.

A group of six special forces troops led Harruhama toward the OMBIcademy entrance. William recognized him immediately, his eyes narrowing at the man. William acted against his strategic impulse and leapt from the rocks onto a short sandy beach ahead of the special forces unit. As he landed, he raised his shotgun and let loose two barrels of explosive pellets, which took down the two leading commandos in a messy burst.

The others moved into the rocks for cover, returning fire as William also moved into cover.

"We just keep running into each other here, don't we, General?" William yelled from behind a rock as he reloaded both barrels.

"Stand aside, Dragoon. I know who you are and have your stepsons held hostage," Harruhama bluffed.

William knew that Connor was with Marlena at least six thousand lightyears away from the beach, and the clash of metal on metal from the titanic struggle above them reminded William where Alex was.

In response to the lie, William grabbed a grenade from his belt and tossed it behind one of the nearby rocks where the enemy troops had taken cover. The explosion knocked them out onto the sand, leaving them stunned and disoriented on the beach. Using the explosion as a distraction, William ran up quickly to where the other two soldiers were hiding. His swift movements won him the first attack and he quickly knocked one of the soldiers to the ground with his shotgun.

The other managed to get up and fire a single round into William's chest. The bullet hurt, but didn't slow him as he smashed the soldier's face with the butt of his shotgun.

William turned to see Harruhama running down the beach away from him. He didn't get far, as William ran him down, grabbing him from behind and throwing him down into the sand.

The general removed his side arm, but William deftly kicked it from his hands.

"I've been waiting for this for a long time," William growled, his eyes narrowing dangerously as he lowered the barrel of his shotgun toward Harruhama.

"You, who betrayed my wife and set my sons to fight each other. You, who tried to kill Connor! It's time for you to pay for what you did to my family!" William yelled, loading his weapon.

"You are a fool, William Mercer. Killing me won't change anything. I only did what I was ordered to do, all of it, from the colonies to your family," Harruhama sobbed.

"Don't lie to me. They were your orders, the great dictator of Earth, the general in charge of the EMC, the subjugator of mankind," William pressed.

"I am a puppet, fool. Mankind has been subjugated for thousands of years. Don't you get it? Everything you call atrocity, every dictator that ever said he was sent by God, they were all His puppets. Only I know the truth because I was the one who found the signal, the one who raised this ship," Harruhama explained, pointing at the OMBIcademy, "the one who has seen the face of Daniel Asher, the messenger of God. I am the one who was chosen to rule mankind forever!"

"I didn't know," William began, lowering his weapon, "that you were completely crazy."

"See for yourself! At the center of the OMBIcademy he has been watching us for two thousand years! You will see!"

—

Alex was gaining ground in the battle. He was beginning to see patterns in Jörmungandr's movements. They were fast and appeared random at first, but the longer the fight went on the more predicable they became.

On one quick striking attack, Alex correctly guessed a feign attack left and let his scimitar dissipate, manifesting a short sword, which he shoved into the gapping maw of the giant serpent, wedging the sword in place. The operative didn't waste the disadvantage and wrapped his ship around Skoll.

"I got you!" the operative called gleefully, allowing Jörmungandr to squeeze Skoll tightly.

A moment later a small explosion from the Nostus caught Alex's attention as he struggled against the pressure. Fenris burst from the fire and flew up to survey the battle raging across the small island.

Alex struggled in vain against the powerful, scaled armor of the serpent as Fenris moved closer.

The large hands of the bigger ship reached out and grabbed the serpent's jaws, pulling them apart, letting the sword fall harmlessly away.

"Uh-oh, Mephisto, time for you to die," the operative teased.

Fenris' hands didn't let go, but continued to pull.

"What are you doing?" the operative screamed.

Vertigo didn't answer, but pulled harder, tearing the mouth of Jörmungandr apart and ripping the snake in half entirely. The cockpit destroyed, the operative had no choice but to eject. The man launched upward, but Skoll was quicker, catching him in midflight.

"Give him to me," Vertigo said after a moment, holding out the broad hands of Fenris.

Alex handed the operative over to his friend who had saved him. He recoiled as Vertigo squeezed tightly and dropped the broken body of the final EMC operative into the ocean below.

"Thanks for helping me, Austin," Alex said, facing the bigger ship.

"I realized I was on the wrong side of this war," Vertigo apologized. "Sorry for hunting you and everything."

"Yeah, don't worry about it. The 4th inhibitor was tricking you. Let's end this war for good," Alex offered.

The two battle suits quickly ended the fight on the rocky coast, by setting down and ordering the surrender of the Nostus' crew.

—

William was leading a defeated Harruhama back toward where the free men had landed on the long landing pad in front of the OMBIcademy. With Skoll and Fenris standing guard, the crew of the Nostus gave up immediately. Their weapons fell to the sand and the fighting was done.

The speaker in William's ear squealed slightly and the voice of Major Edmund Sanders came through, on the edge of hysteria.

"Anyone outside the OMBIcademy, retreat immediately, we have a problem in here!" he called.

"Major Sanders, this is Mephisto, what is the problem, over?" Alex's asked.

"I think this old ship is taking off! Pull back!" Sanders cried.

Alex took control, issuing quick orders for everyone to board transports and get off the island. Shortly after the evacuation began, the entire island began to rumble as men ran toward their transports.

"It's him! I told you! He won't let you fools have Earth!" Harruhama yelled as the ground began to crack.

William moved quickly, handing off Harruhama to Commander Weiss near one of the transports.

"Don't let him go! He needs to pay for what he's done!" William yelled, turning back toward the OMBIcademy.

"What are you going to do?" Weiss yelled back.

"William, don't!" Alex's voice cried through the communicator.

"This has to stop! We need to find a way to stop it! I'll try to get a cargo port open for you, Alex, but for now, get these people away from here," William said as he began running toward the lone door at the far end of the landing pad.

He covered the ground quickly, dodging fissures that were opening on the concrete as he ran. When he neared the OMBIcademy he pulled the keycard out of his pocket. He got to the door and frantically waved the card in front of the door. The door opened as the OMBIcademy began to separate from the landing pad and lift off the ground. William dove through the opening in a roll, coming to a stop in the cold gray halls of the OMBIcademy.

———

Marlena stood in the observation room, holding her son close while her three companions searched.

Artemis scanned with her OMBI carefully while Anataur dove into the flooded room, disappearing into the dark water.

"Is he for real?" Ethan asked.

Artemis grinned. "Oh yeah. He's alone in there, I'm tracking him on thermal."

Anataur emerged nearly two minutes later, frowning.

"That's cold!" he whined, climbing to the edge. Artemis was waiting to help him out.

"Well?" Marlena asked.

"Nothing down there that I saw," Anataur said, climbing back to the observation deck.

"They must be in one of the dark areas," Artemis said, pointing.

Marlena laid Connor down upon one of the strange blocks, which seemed to contour to his shape, and peered into the darkness to the right of the lift.

"I can't see a thing," she whispered after a moment.

"I can. There are some pretty big thermal readings coming from in there, and more movement on my motion sensor than I can account for with heat signatures," Artemis said.

"What about the other room?" she asked, keeping her voice soft, below the sound of collapsing walls and angry beasts.

"Nothing moving in there." Artemis let her vision cycle from infrared to thermal. "That is, nothing I can see. There is some kind of tree-like canopy in the way to get a real good look."

Compared to the other rooms, the treed dark room was quiet. The sound of the wind rustling through trees made it seem almost serene.

"Motion?" Marlena asked Artemis, who only shook her head.

Marlena moved to climb down, when Anataur stopped her with a strong hand on her shoulder.

"Come on, I know you want to help your son, but you can't see down there. Let us go," he said, nodding to Artemis who was already climbing in.

Marlena reluctantly nodded, stepping aside to wait next to her son.

Ethan waited, rifle drawn. His eyes scanned the broken windows intently.

—

Inside the room, Anataur and Artemis descended below the tree canopy to see a soft glow from their infrared vision. The moss gave off the odd light, which they couldn't see from above, as it was invisible to the naked eye. The landscape was that of a thick forest and was eerily quiet.

Artemis and Anataur stayed close together, looking around for a discarded OMBI. Near the center of the room, they could hear a slight humming sound and saw a metal crate half buried in the moss.

"Is this it?" Anataur whispered.

"I don't know. Let's open it and find out," Artemis suggested.

The two friends knelt at the crate and first tried to lift it, but couldn't find a good enough grip to budge the heavy crate.

"Just open it," Artemis suggested.

In response Anataur manifested his oversized hammer and swung at the corner as hard as he could. The crate didn't open, but a large dent remained where he had hit it. He continued to strike until it finally gave, cracking open and revealing glowing from the inside.

Artemis moved forward and reached her hand deep inside the crack and grabbed a metallic object inside. From the crate she removed a large strip of smooth, flexible metal. Neither had seen an OMBI that wasn't modified by the UEDF or on someone's wrist. It looked extremely different from the ones they wore. One side was completely smooth with no interface or motherboard for the inhibitor chips, the other side had several, inch long spikes protruding in a line down the center.

For a moment, they weren't sure if it was even an OMBI, but it was the right size and both of them remembered the pain in their arm when they first awoke with an OMBI in place.

"I guess this is it," Artemis said, turning it over in her hand.

"I'm not sure, but it's something. Let's go back," Anataur replied uncertainly.

They all but ran to the edge of the battle room, carefully climbing the uneven wall until they were back in the observation room. Ethan was waiting at the edge and helped them over the threshold. Marlena's eagerness was visible on her face as they walked over to her and handed her the strange device.

"This is it?" she whispered.

"We're not sure, but we think so," Artemis shrugged.

Marlena took the metal strip and held it toward Connor's bare right arm, pressing the spikes gently against his skin.

"I'm not sure I can do it," she said, hesitating.

As it turned out, she didn't have to. The spikes, upon making contact with the boy's skin, dug themselves deeply into his forearm as the metal device wrapped itself around, giving Connor a second smooth, metal bracer.

The boy's chocolate-brown eyes shot open immediately upon connecting with the uninhibited device. He looked straight up and blinked several times before grabbing his own head with both hands and screaming.

Anataur immediately spun toward the first dark room, hammer appearing in his waiting hands. Artemis reacted quickly, arrow nocked before the bow had even fully appeared, aiming toward the other inhabited room's broken window. Marlena and Ethan both stepped back, surprised, and looked around frantically.

"Oh my boy, what have I done?!" Marlena cried.

The boy began to convulse wildly, his eyes shut tight. He thrashed and fell off the block he was lying on. Marlena quickly ran to his side, trying to steady the flailing boy.

Hearing a roar from the dark room, Ethan picked up his rifle and took aim.

"We have to go!" he said, firing a round at a large gnarled hand that grabbed the ledge, sending the rest of the beast crashing down into the room.

He reloaded quickly, taking another shot at the next figure to appear. The noise of the rifle had caught the attention of the creatures in the other room as well, and soon arachni-bears leapt onto the ledge into a hail of black arrows.

Not to be left out, Anataur moved toward the ledge of the dark room and began swinging at the large grasping hands.

"These are reapers!" he yelled, as he swung at another.

Marlena steadied herself through the frantic yelling and grabbed her son's shoulders, holding him down against his convulsing.

"Connor," she whispered, "I know you can hear me. We need your help, baby. Please wake up!"

Connor stopped shaking immediately. His eyes popped open, glowing with a soft shade of brown light as he looked at Marlena's face.

Anataur slammed against the block beside Connor and Marlena, blood flowing from his nose as black armor began to form around his body. He shook his head back and forth as he got up, running back toward the reapers.

"Mom?" Connor asked, blinking several times as tears began to rim his eyes.

"Yes, baby, I'm here," Marlena said, holding Connor tightly, tears forming in her eyes.

Ethan fired one shot and spun as the hot shell ejected backwards over his shoulder, quickly loading and firing another round in the opposite direction. Artemis stopped trying to be stealthy and began firing explosive arrows into the arachni-bears, sending them scurrying over the edge.

"Am I dreaming?" Connor asked, reaching up to touch her face.

"No, my sweet boy, you're not. We're both awake. But we need to get out of here, right now. Can you help us?"

Connor closed his eyes, taking a deep breath. The lights went on in the observation room, glowing brightly as Connor inhaled and dimming as he exhaled.

Anataur was at the edge, swinging furiously, when a clawed hand wrapped around his leg, pulling him into the darkness and the reapers waiting below.

Artemis ran in his direction as fast as her OMBI-enhanced

speed would carry her, firing explosive arrows into the climbing reapers as she ran.

"Anataur, shield!" she yelled, reaching the ledge, manifesting her own shield. She dropped her bow, which dissipated before it hit the ground, and in her hands appeared two grenades, which she immediately threw into the room, followed by two more and two more after that. She kept throwing until the first pair exploded then dove back, avoiding the claw of a climbing reaper.

The room lit up with several pairs of explosions. Anataur was knocked around as he focused on keeping his shield up. The reapers were tough, but even so the explosives knocked them hard around the room, leaving many of them unable to walk right, shrapnel lodged deeply into their thick hides.

Connor opened his eyes and looked at his two bracers.

"I hear you, Omega." He smiled.

He nodded to himself and stood up as if he hadn't been asleep for weeks. The bracer on his left hand even looked better, metal reforming into clean lines.

Looking at Marlena, Connor held out his right hand. "That's Muriel, she's healing Omega for me. She's a Cryptolith. So is Omega. The ghost of one, anyway."

Marlena nodded slowly, trying to focus on her son as several screamers began wailing, trying to gain a foothold on the ledge near the malfunctioning room.

"Last shot!" Ethan yelled, firing it into the eyeless face of a screamer. He dropped his rifle and drew a long knife from his belt, stepping in front of Marlena and Connor.

Connor continued talking to himself as he moved, dashing around the room. Uninhibited and using the power of two OMBIs, Connor ran toward the screamers, punching and kicking at them. He landed several heavy blows, which caused the first of the screamers to explode in a horrible popping sound. The gore didn't touch Connor as two more were destroyed in rapid succession. He blinked to the other side of the room nearly faster than Marlena could follow. He slammed into the reaper that had been about to grab Artemis and rode its falling body down into the dark room. The lights came on as he landed, jumping off the broken body of the pig-faced creature.

He landed between Anataur and three bleeding reapers that were surrounding him. Connor stepped back slightly, so he was right beside the larger boy.

"Let's get these guys!" Connor nodded to Anataur, who grinned and nodded back.

Connor ran straight between two of them, kicking out in two directions, connecting hard with both their snouted faces, causing their tusks to snap under the weight of the hit.

Anataur used the distraction and brought his hammer down into the face of the third one that already had one arm hanging limply at its side.

The two Connor hit fell and tried to get back up, until Connor jumped on one and kicked it in the jaw, causing a loud snapping sound to echo in the room. Anataur was on the other immediately, hitting it several times with his heavy hammer until it stopped moving.

The threat neutralized, Connor ran to the center of the room and linked his fingers together, looking at Anataur and nodding to the ledge above. Trusting the strength of the kid, Anataur ran toward him and was vaulted to the ledge, where Artemis caught him and wrapped him in a tight hug.

"You big, stupid dummy, don't do that again!" she scolded, wiping what Anataur thought was a tear from her face.

Connor urged the battle room to create some steps for him and bounded his way back up using the rocks that jutted from the ground. They fell away as he jumped to the ledge, smiling.

"I have to admit, this is fun." Connor beamed.

Marlena wrapped him in a tight hug. The beasts that were

left began retreating back into their rooms and, with the threat diminishing, Connor let the tears fall from his face.

"I saw you die so many times in my dreams, Mom. I never thought I'd ever get to see you again," he sobbed, hugging Marlena.

Marlena cried too.

"I tried to come get you but I couldn't make it. I'm so sorry. So much has happened," she said as her tears wet her cheeks.

"I know, Omega told me," Connor said suddenly, wiping the tears from his eyes. "I have to go, Mom."

"Where? Let's get out of here first," Marlena said, still sobbing.

"No. I called Hati, he's already coming. He thinks he can get through the storm," Connor explained. "I am going to go stop the UEDF fleet from attacking Aeris VII."

"Connor, there are more than seventy frigates. Hati is strong, but not that strong," Marlena said, the worry clear in her voice.

"Hati is as strong as I am, and I am very strong," Connor replied as he tightened his fists.

Connor took a step then stopped and looked at Ethan and blinked several times.

"Hi, Dad," he said simply.

"Hi, Connor," Ethan waved, a grin appearing on his face.

"You two," Connor said, looking at Anataur and Artemis, "Take my mom to Earth. William and Alex need her help. They're tough, but I don't think they can win without her. I'll be there as soon as I can."

Connor activated his locate function, drawing a line, the shortest distance between him and Alex.

He nodded toward their wrists.

"There, you can now locate Alex too. The training rooms are connected between the Aesir, uh, the OMBIcademies. It's a long way, but once you're in, you can use your vehicles. Hurry, okay?" Connor asked, stepping toward the door to the anteroom.

The ship rumbled and they heard the faint sound of a crashing somewhere above them.

"I see the line. Okay, we'll take care of it, little man." Anataur nodded.

"Don't call me that, fatso," Connor barked back as he walked out to the empty elevator shaft.

"I'll see you soon," Marlena called after him.

"See you soon, Mom." Connor smiled as he jumped up from ledge to ledge up the elevator shaft.

CHAPTER 10

Level 99

T HE HALLWAYS OF THE OMBICADEMY WERE DARK BUT William waited, letting his eyes adjust to the faint lighting. The ship was moving, he knew, but it didn't feel very different from when it was sitting still. He could hear men yelling far off down the halls, most likely free men who had entered the structure before the lockdown to subdue the guards.

"Alex, can you hear me?" William asked into his communicator.

"Yeah, you okay?" Alex replied.

William shut his eyes and took a deep breath, glad he could still communicate with his stepson.

"Yes, I'm fine. It's a little dark in here, just letting my eyes adjust. What does it look like out there?" William asked.

"Check it out," Alex replied.

William removed the datapad from his pocket and found Alex streaming a video feed. The OMBIcademy was rising from the island. It wasn't a disc shape like William had thought it would be but, instead, a large cone with multiple tiers protruding at various levels.

"Alex, pan down to where it was before," William said.

Alex complied. Below the OMBIcademy, ocean water was

quickly filling the hole that had been left by the huge structure. It had been rooted into the ground, partially in the sea.

"Pretty weird, eh?" Alex asked.

"Yeah, the saltwater didn't tarnish it at all. Keep up the evacuation, I'll find a way to open a cargo hold or something for you if I can. I am going to try to find Major Sanders," William explained, finally being able to see.

"Okay, I will. Keep me updated and be careful," Alex said quickly.

William walked into the OMBIcademy, wandering down the halls he had only been in once before, several months earlier. He had been so heavily medicated at that time, he didn't remember his way around very well.

The halls were like a catacomb, many crossing hallways leading to doors that wouldn't open for William's key card. There were a fair amount of dead ends and William quickly decided that he was lost.

"Alex, how did you get around in the OMBIcademy? It's like a maze," William all but whispered.

"Oh, our OMBI always would point to our barracks and eventually I learned my way around. Just keep going, it's not really that big. At least, that level isn't that big," Alex replied.

William smirked. He had forgotten his communicator was active and hadn't really meant to ask Alex for directions. The advice Alex gave was good though and before long William found a lift where a trio of confused free men were standing.

"Hey, what is the status here?" William asked.

Turning toward him the men looked him up and down before one replied.

"We secured the facility and all the kids are in their barracks. We are standing guard here now for Asher until we get ordered somewhere else," the man informed in a monotonous voice, sounding slightly confused.

"Okay. Do you know where I can find Major Sanders?" William asked, unsure of what the guard was talking about.

"No, he might be upstairs or in his quarters, maybe he is in with some of the kids," the man answered while staring at a wall.

"Got it," William said, wanting to get away from the confused men. "Where is Blue Army's barracks?"

The man pointed down the hallway, opposite where William had come from. William didn't think that the man knew where he was, let alone where William wanted to go, but he followed the direction anyway and after a few wrong turns found the door marked with a blue sea serpent.

William used the butt of his shotgun and pounded on the door and waited until the door opened slightly, a young teenager looking at him expectantly.

"Is Amanda here? From the class of 2126?" William asked, figuring that starting with one of the two people in the OMBIcademy who knew him would be better than just wandering around.

"Who wants to know?" the boy asked skeptically.

"I am Connor's, uh, Raptor's stepdad," William offered, hoping the name would spark recognition.

"Come in! Come in!" the boy said, opening the door for him.

Inside, many of the soldiers from Blue Army were talking quietly in the common room of the barracks. The dark-haired boy who answered the door introduced himself as "Flayer," then led William to the 2126 barracks and pointed inside.

The kids in the long room were, for the most part, sitting on their bunks playing with their datapads. A few had been talking quietly when he entered, all heads turning toward him.

"William?" the girl's voice asked.

Her thick, Irish accent was unmistakable.

"Hey, Amanda, can I talk to you?" he replied.

She nodded, cocking her head to the side. "Everyone, this is William Mercer, Connor's stepdad who I told you about. He is the Dragoon who started the free men Revolution," she said, walking over to him.

The children in the room all seemed to get excited and walked over to inspect the leader of a revolution.

"Uh, the revolution is over, actually. We won. General Harruhama was taken into custody today, in fact," William informed as the kids surrounded him.

"What? That's great. Does that mean Connor is going to come back?" Amanda pressed.

"I'm not sure. He got hurt in a battle, in space. His mom actually found him and took him to get better. I haven't heard from them in a while, but I'm sure they're okay." Uncertainty was evident in his tone.

"His mom? I thought his mom was the Phoenix?" a blond-haired kid asked in a southern accent.

"Yeah, that's right. She has been leading the Independent Colonies for the last six years," William said to the skeptical faces before adding, "I thought she was dead too."

That statement caused a murmur throughout the room. Everyone knew the story of the Incident of 2115 and many of them idolized Marlena.

"Oh," Amanda said, sounding worried. "What are you doing here anyway?"

"I came with a group of free men to liberate the OMBIcademy and apprehend Harruhama. We got him outside but then the OMBIcademy closed up and, well, it's flying right now. I'm looking for Major Sanders, do you know where he is?" William asked.

The children of Blue Army 2126 seemed quite shocked at the news and began talking amongst themselves. Amanda tapped her OMBI several times then stared off in the distance for a moment.

"He is above us, probably in the observation lounge or in his quarters. Do you want me to send him a message and find out?" Amanda asked smartly.

"Why didn't I think of that? Yes. Then message me and tell me where to meet him. Tell him I am looking for him, okay?" William said, patting Amanda on the shoulder.

William turned to go and Amanda caught him by the hand.

"Is Connor really okay?" she asked, sounding like a kid for the first time in the conversation.

"I don't know. I hope so, Amanda," William offered.

Leaving the barracks, William had one of the kids from Blue Army open the door for him back into the hallway. Heading back the way he had come from, he quickly arrived at the lift to see the same three men standing guard.

William walked passed them and pressed the button, calling the lift.

"What are you doing?" one of the men asked.

"I'm going upstairs," William replied as if it was obvious.

"Not to the observation room, right?" the man asked again, gripping his rifle.

"Nope, officer's quarters," William answered quickly.

"Okay, don't go further than that. You're not allowed in there." The man turned back to face the wall.

The door closed shut just as his datapad buzzed.

-*Message received*-

To: William Mercer

Subject: Sanders

Message: Room 17, Blue door, officer's quarters."

"Thank you, Amanda," William said to the datapad.

Getting off in the officer's quarters, William walked down the hall, stopping at the blue door, and knocked.

The door opened to reveal a tired-looking Major Sanders, who eyed William suspiciously.

"What are you doing here?" Sanders asked.

"I got aboard just as the OMBIcademy took off; we got your warning. What happened?" William asked.

"First, tell me what you think of Asher," Sanders ordered, one hand resting on the sidearm on his hip.

"I don't know who that is. Harruhama mentioned him too, said he was a messenger of God and has been on Earth for two thousand years. So, I guess I don't really think of him at all," William answered honestly.

Sanders visibly relaxed and pulled William into his quarters.

"You're not under its influence yet. Good," Sanders said quickly.

"What is going on, Major?" William asked.

"I don't have all the details, but as the UEDF started falling apart from your revolution, Harruhama started acting stranger and eventually seemed to snap. As soon as he disappeared the officers here started talking about Asher and something called a Xudok. I locked the children in their barracks and went up to talk to Colonel Setzer about it, but he was worst of all," Sanders explained, talking quickly.

"You told me he was losing it when you let the free men in. What did he say, specifically?" William asked calmly.

"That same stuff about a messenger of God and how he was going to live forever if he obeyed. There is something messing with people's minds here and it seems to target certain people over others. My hypothesis is, it goes after people who take orders easily, first. People like you, who are completely defiant of authority, are more resistant to it. I am not entirely unaffected but I have been able to resist so far. The kids don't seem to be effected yet, but I don't know for how much longer."

"So what is it, some kind of alien that has been living in this ship, controlling Harruhama for thirty-five years, and trying to rule the world?" William asked.

"I think that is exactly it." Sanders shook his head in disbelief.

"Why?" William asked simply. "What is the end game for something like that? I can kind of understand the temptation of living forever for old men like Harruhama, but what would an alien need to use up Earth for, or the colonies for that matter?"

"I just don't have the answer," Sanders said.

William raised his hand to his chin and began to pace around the room.

"They said that they found a second ship like this on another planet. Maybe it was about finding that ship or another one of its own kind. It needed humanity to develop slipstream drives and colonize worlds, not for the resources, but to find something," William hypothesized carefully.

Major Sanders shrugged.

"Major, is there any way we can get to wherever Asher is? I also told Alex that I'd open a cargo bay for him if I could. Can you help me?" William asked, looking Sanders in the eye.

"We may be able to open a bay from the observation deck or the control room. I don't know where Asher is but, with the way Colonel Setzer was acting, he might know. Let's go, I'll take you up there," Sanders said, walking into the hall.

"William. Something weird is happening out here," Alex said on the open com, stopping William and Sanders.

"What is it, Alex?"

"The evacuation is complete but a bunch of UEDF fighters just flew in and have been circling the OMBIcademy. I got close to one and it tried to shoot me. William, they have no pilots. They're all on remote control or something and there are more coming," Alex said.

William and Major Sanders shared a worried glance and began to hurry down the hall toward the lift.

—

The walk back to the training room went quickly but, inside, the landscaped had changed. There was no longer a house but what looked like an ancient Roman city. Anataur led the group slowly into the room, following the line on his OMBI as it pointed down the cobbled street. Artemis followed, keeping her keen eyes on the windows above.

Marlena and Ethan followed them into the strange city, leaving behind the nightmare of Dytopa II. Marlena didn't like leaving her son to climb around the infested ship alone, but she trusted in him and the confidence in his eyes reassured her that he would be all right.

The air was chilly and the streets seemed abandoned. It quickly became clear that the pathway was suspended on what looked like a cloud. Breaks in the clouds below showed a rocky coastline and an ocean several thousand feet below them.

"So, this is some kind of cloud city?" Ethan asked, shocked.

"The training rooms all have a different setting. I've seen stranger things than this," Artemis confessed, not taking her eyes from the building to their left.

She stopped suddenly and quietly said, "We aren't alone, someone is watching us."

"Keep walking, it might be your imagination," Anataur replied, trying not to look at the buildings.

"It isn't," she replied sternly.

Marlena gripped her side arm, ejecting the magazine and counting how many bullets she had.

"Seventeen," she muttered in reply to Ethan's inquisitive look.

"Better than me," he said, holding his short knife in one hand.

"Connor said that Omega was part of his OMBI and manifested in the training rooms; maybe you guys can manifest your OMBI Cryptolith ghosts to help you too," Marlena offered, grimacing at how strange it sounded to her.

Anataur turned and looked at Artemis, who took her eyes off the buildings to look back at him.

"I don't know," Artemis shrugged. "I've never heard of that happening until he said something about it. We always did the tests our teachers gave us."

Movement from the building Artemis had been staring at caught Marlena's eye.

"There's something here, everyone, be on your guard," she warned.

As if in response, a strange female voice spoke seemingly from nowhere. It said simply, "Training activated, virtual army engaged."

From the buildings, armored Roman troops began to pour out by the dozens.

"Oh come on!" Anataur yelled, manifesting his large hammer.

Artemis chuckled and began to manifest her bow, letting arrow after arrow fly. Some detonated in the middle of groups of soldiers, while others picked off individuals that moved to flank them. The remaining virtual enemies charged forward fearlessly but were easily defeated by Anataur's hammer.

"Level two," the voice said, as archers began to take positions on the windows.

"How many levels are there?" Ethan asked aloud as arrows began to fly in, forcing the unarmored man to take cover. One arrow struck Marlena's arm, but bounced harmlessly off her battle suit.

"...levels remaining," the broken voice said as if answering Ethan directly.

"Uh, end training!" he said back.

"Invalid command," the voice answered as arrows began to rain down, causing Anataur and Artemis to bring up their armor and shields. Even Marlena took cover after deflecting another arrow with her armor.

"Come on! Skip level two!" Ethan called out, trying to figure out how to make the haywire machine stop.

"Level three," the voice said as the arrows dissipated and the archers faded from sight.

The ground rumbled up and down the cobbled street as a group of cavalry appeared, riding hard toward them.

"Stop it!" Marlena yelled at Ethan.

"No, it should let us skip to the highest level attained so far!" Artemis yelled. "Go right to that one, and if we can beat it, the simulation should end!"

"Are you sure?" Marlena called back.

Artemis shrugged at her before turning and firing a pair of arrows at the advancing horse-mounted soldiers.

"Okay," Ethan began, "skip to final level!"

"Level ninety-nine," the voice said ominously.

"Crap," Anataur said as the cavalry men faded away.

"There," Marlena said as a large claw appeared at the edge of the floating island behind them.

The great red dragon lifted itself over the edge, towering above the buildings, and looked down at the four companions, smiling broadly, showing off its long sword-like teeth.

—

Connor hopped out of the elevator shaft into a group of waiting arachni-bears, which had apparently heard the commotion below. They charged, reaching for the boy, but he dashed around them, running up the wall and jumping off over the first and then beneath the eight legs of the next. He continued his run down the hallway, ignoring the enemies. The quick beasts howled as they gave chase behind him.

Their nearly invisible webs were placed at regular intervals in the hall and Connor purposely ran straight into them. He manifested two daggers, one that glowed blue and the other shimmering silver as he spun, cutting through the webs before rolling out the large crack in the side of the ship, into the waiting arms of Hati.

"Welcome back, Initiator," Hati growled in Connor's mind, the full sound of its voice causing Connor to smile broadly.

Uninhibited, Connor could hear every word clearly and let Hati share all the information it had gathered with him. The information exchange was seamless, Connor's mind opening to the data like he was reading a book. While they traded stories and information, Connor crawled into the suit, where he sat comfortably and began to unlock all of Hati's weaponry, abilities, and equipment.

"Thank you, Hati. It's nice to see you again too," Connor said aloud, greeting his friend.

Connor spent a few moments suspended in his vessel, going through his OMBI menu and unlocking everything that had been locked before, including several new weapon trees that hadn't been there the last time he looked.

The storm outside raged, the strange orange lightning striking Hati several times. The ship didn't seem to mind though, and to Connor, it felt like Hati was enjoying the act of defying the powerful storm. All around them strange herds of beasts looked up at the ship. A few strange projectiles hit various places around Hati, including one large rock that a huge, white-haired giant threw at it. But Connor just sat, unnerved, watching the strange scene around him.

"Where is the invasion fleet?" Connor asked to Omega and Muriel after a few moments of studying the beasts below him.

"They are currently in slipstream on their way to Aeris VII," they answered together, their masculine and feminine voices harmonizing perfectly.

Connor willed Hati higher into the air, looking down at an endless sea of strange monster herds until he pierced the cloud barrier. It was hard to see for a moment but they quickly reached the other side, where a peaceful night above the storm awaited them. The white dwarf star that Dytopa II orbited was on the opposite side of the planet and Connor could see into the eternity of the night above.

"Look, everyone, today I'm a hero," Connor mumbled to himself, earning a gleeful response from the three entities that rode beside him.

"Omega, have Tizona follow us back, Mom will want her ship back home when she gets there," Connor said as they lifted out into orbit.

"Affirmative, Initiator."

The other ship responded to the call and met Hati in Orbit. Connor smiled as his mom's Anubis fighter flew beside him. He had never seen it personally, but had watched it get destroyed a hundred times in his dreams. Watching it drift so close, Connor reminded himself that his mom and William were alive, and if he could move quick enough, they would stay alive. Connor focused on that thought and created a slipstream to Aeris VII.

———

William and Major Sanders stood patiently in the lift as it ascended up to the observation lounge.

"This is the slowest lift I have ever been on," William remarked, leaning against the wall.

Major Sanders just shrugged, having grown used to the slow progression. The lift behaved strangely, taking as much time to go up or down three levels as it did one level, as if the time taken were the determining factor of the elevation rather than the destination.

The door eventually opened to reveal the anteroom in disarray. The administrator sat staring at the wall, mumbling to herself about being young and attractive forever and ignored the men as they crossed the room until they reached the door. She glanced at them as they opened it, without speaking to them, and went back to her quiet muttering when they had gone through.

The observation lounge remained as it had before the change, largely untouched. Colonel Setzer was sitting at his desk, looking at his datapad, when they walked in. The stocky bald man looked up at them expectantly when they got to his desk.

"Hello, Sanders, who is this?" Setzer asked, acting surprisingly lucid.

"This is William, Connor Pereira's stepfather," Sanders said, introducing the man.

"Then you're here to get revenge for what we did to that kid," Setzer assumed aloud while standing up.

"What do you mean?" William's eyes narrowed dangerous at the implication.

"Oh, well, he needed to be taken down a peg, the little

brat. So we taught him a lesson is all. I didn't know that Black Squadron kid would hospitalize him."

William's lip curled in a slight snarl and he looked at Major Sanders for confirmation. The Major took a deep breath before nodding affirmatively.

"Actually, we're looking for Mr. Asher, Harruhama sent us to talk to…" Sanders began before being cut off.

"Harruhama! Ha! His days are done. I am the chosen one now! Only I get to speak to the voice of God! So anything you have to say to Mr. Asher, you can say to me!" Colonel Setzer interrupted.

"Okay then," William began deliberately, "stop what you're doing. Surrender and we won't be forced to kill you."

A sigh escaped Sander's lips as Colonel Setzer leapt over his desk at William. The man was strong and no stranger to a brawl, but William's enhanced strength and speed easily turned away the charging man's momentum, sending him tumbling into a nearby table, cracking it in half.

Setzer wasn't finished and broke off a table leg, using it as a club, swinging hard at William, who deflected the blow with an upraised arm. The battle went on for nearly a minute, Setzer playing through the momentum of his initial charge, panting heavily when William grabbed the larger man and pinned him to the ground.

"Where is Asher?" William asked, holding the man's arm tightly behind his back.

"I'll never tell you!" Setzer yelled defiantly.

William pulled the man's arm upward, causing Colonel Setzer to groan in pain.

"What use is immortality if you can't use your arms?" William asked in a cold tone.

"The center of the OMBIcademy, down the tube," Setzer said weakly, nodding slightly to the wall behind his desk.

William let the man up slowly as Major Sanders inspected the wall. After a few moments, Sanders had the secret door open, pulling on a small lever behind a painting of a lotus flower.

"Daniel Asher is the voice of God. What will you possibly do to him?" Setzer began before William leveled him with a punch to the face, knocking the large man back onto the ground.

The man looked up at William in time to see the butt of a shotgun connect with his forehead.

"That's for Connor," William remarked quietly, turning his shotgun around in his hands.

"You'd murder him?" Sanders asked as William hesitated.

"No, I'm just trying to decide if he is too dangerous to be left alive."

"Let's decide that after we deal with the man that is manipulating his mind. He's not a good man but I don't know if he deserves death," Sanders said, surprising himself by his compassion.

"Fine," William finally agreed.

The two men entered the tube apprehensively, which immediately began descending.

"Alex, I'm headed down toward the bottom center of the OMBIcademy," William said.

"Roger. There are a lot of unmanned fighters out here now. The ship has begun moving off to the west, also. It's going pretty fast," Alex said, updating William.

"Understood, I'll keep in touch."

—

Outside the OMBIcademy, the situation was a little different than Alex described. Several frigates from the 1st fleet had begun coming into orbit and surrounding the OMBIcademy ship. Their unmanned fighters flew in intricate patterns, attacking Alex and Austin whenever they got too close. The ship had begun moving west as Alex said, but it was going so quickly and Alex struggled to keep up while also trying to disable enemy ships.

Fenris and Skoll made a good team, using Skoll's speed and Fenris' strength to take down RA fighters quickly. Both of them had full armor and shields in place, and despite being severely outnumbered, they were making progress against the enemy fleet.

Things got more difficult when the frigates begun firing upon them. The shots from the heavy cannons were slow and predicable but it made keeping up harder.

"We should take down those frigates," Austin suggested, while firing several small missiles at a squadron of RA fighters that had broken off from the swarm.

On an open channel Alex said, "Frigates of the 1st fleet, this is Mephisto of Black Squadron, stand down and cease your attack."

"Captain Mephisto, we are unable to access our systems. Something is controlling our ship," a crewmen from one of the frigates answered.

"Well, we can't kill innocent people," Austin said somberly.

"It's worse than that, Austin. What could possibly be controlling all these ships like this?" Alex wondered.

Austin was silent.

"Yeah, I don't know either," Alex said, spinning in a defensive roll away from heavy cannon fire.

More Frigates appeared above and Alex figured that the entire 1st fleet was coming in to escort the OMBIcademy to wherever it was going.

Alex grew more concerned and, while dodging the cannons of an unmanned Anubis fighter, plotted the course of the OMBIcademy.

"Austin, this thing is heading straight toward North America, do you know where it's going?" Alex asked, sending the map and trajectory to his friend.

"Let's see. The only place I see that it could be headed is the

Orbital Defense Grid Control Center in Cheyenne Mountain, Colorado," Austin said confidently.

"Are you sure?" Alex asked.

"Yeah, I learned about it in my operative training," Austin explained.

"Okay, let's try to slow this fleet down, we don't want whatever is controlling it to get a hold of the orbital defenses. If it does, humanity could go extinct in a matter of days," Alex said.

As an afterthought Alex contacted the free men leaders, getting as many of them on his communicator as he could.

"This is Captain Alex Pereira, many of you know me already. Right now I am in pursuit of an alien spacecraft that is headed toward the Orbital Defense Grid controls in Cheyenne Mountain, Colorado. The entire 1st fleet is being controlled by the ship and at its current rate of speed we anticipate that we have no more than six hours. Anyone who can reach the coordinates that follow, bring whatever armament you have to defend this site. We cannot let our enemy take control of the orbital defense grid!" Alex commanded, sending coordinates.

"Okay, Austin, let's buy them some time," Alex said, manifesting large cannons on both arms of Skoll.

"Roger," Austin said, firing another barrage of missiles.

—

Anataur drove recklessly fast over the rough stone. He had manifested an AX-11 and forced himself to concentrate on keeping his manifestation whole as he drove. Ethan sat beside him, calling out obstacles as large stone slabs rained down from the buildings being destroyed behind them.

Marlena felt helpless in the backseat, watching the scene unfold around her. The red dragon was crawling after them, violently destroying the floating city in its wake. She had no idea how to defeat such a massive beast. So she sat, holding Artemis' legs while she stood up in the vehicle out the open sunroof, firing arrow after arrow at the pursuer.

Artemis' short tan hair flung around wildly in the wind as she continued her barrage. He had tried aiming for the eyes at first but the dragon was too quick for that, closing his armored eyelids, turning his head or swiping the arrows away. The armor seemed impenetrable. She switched to explosive arrows, which popped into small puffs of smoke, not slowing the creature at all.

She used every arrow in her arsenal, armor piercing, which bit deep but didn't penetrate the scales. Her nets caused the creature to laugh as they tangled themselves in the scales and hung awkwardly before Artemis let the manifestation go. She rotated incendiary, ice, trip line, and watched as they all failed to slow the beast.

She dropped her bow as Anataur made a sharp turn to avoid a falling slab, forcing it to rematerialize in her hand a moment later. She had nearly run out of ideas when she pulled back on the string and manifested a lightning arrow. Normally used for stunning or hindering electronics, she rarely produced it because she would often zap her own fingers holding the string if she waited too long to release.

The small lightning bolt struck the creature's nose, which made it roar as it flinched.

"Its weakness is electrical attacks!" Artemis called out to Anataur, who didn't look away from the road.

He was following the black line on the road from his OMBI's return function, trusting that Connor wasn't misleading him. Artemis continued to unleash a string of lightning strikes as fast as she could pull back her bow string. The dragon dodged down a side road, leaving a trail of dust and destruction to avoid the stinging arrows.

"I won't be able to stop it with these," Artemis said, sitting back down in the vehicle.

"Try combining your bow with something bigger!" Anataur advised, shouting above the screeching of the wheels.

Out of the corner of her eyes Marlena noticed the dragon taking flight, lifting off the ground easily and moving ahead of the AX-11.

"It's flying and coming around in front of us!" Marlena called out.

Artemis cycled through her OMBI menu in her mind as quickly as she could, wondering what weapons a bow could pair with. Bow and sniper rifle would make a scoped crossbow. Bow and shotgun would create a spread shot dart launcher. Bow and machinegun would be an auto-crossbow.

"None of these combinations will help!" Artemis called out.

"Not weapons! Unlock an assault vehicle and try that!" Anataur called out as the dragon landed ahead of them.

Anataur almost let his manifestation fail as the dragon reared back its head and blew a line of fire at the AX-11. He managed to get his shield up in time, which quickly began to weaken in the flames. The boy was sweating intensely as he raised armor around the vehicle just as the shield faded. The AX-11 got hot quickly and Anataur turned away blindly, colliding with a half-broken pillar.

The AX-11 spun in circles until it hit the edge of a fountain and flipped into the water.

Anataur let it dissipate immediately, leaving the four sitting in the water of a large fountain. Shaking off their dizziness. The group ran forward into a large columned building as the dragon clawed around the corner and crawled after them.

Realizing that they couldn't escape, Anataur stopped on the steps and turned to face the massive beast while the others ran.

"How did such a weak little lizard get to be the level ninety-nine boss? What is this, a training room for babies?!" he taunted, trying to draw the dragon's attention. The creature took the bait and began to track Anataur with its eyes, following his movements as he walked up to the opposite side of the fountain.

The dragon was halfway through the water when it realized its mistake. At the top of the steps, Artemis aimed the ballista carefully at the dragon's feet and released a huge lightning bolt into the water.

The dragon's muscles seized and caused it to collapse. His long neck had the misfortune of landing near Anataur, who dashed forward with his oversized hammer, charging the end with electrical energy. He swung the hammer down heavily between the dragon's eyes.

The dragon tried to stand, but another ballista shot took it in the side, causing it to collapse back down to the ground. Timing stunning shot and hammer swing, the two friends continued their vicious attack for what seemed like several minutes. Anataur, even with his endurance and strength enhanced by his OMBI, felt exhausted when the dragon finally stopped moving. The red scales on its side were blackened with the scorch marks of the huge lightning arrows. The skull had cracked and dark blood oozed from the thing's eyes and nose.

After a moment the dragon dissipated and the training room reset itself, reforming the buildings around them.

"Yes!" Artemis called out, running down the steps to Anataur, who spun her around when she jumped into his arms.

"We rock!" she said, smiling at her best friend.

"Nice move with the ballista; looks like a fun new toy," Anataur congratulated.

Marlena and Ethan moved to join the two enthusiastic friends, who seemed very much like teenagers just then.

"Congratulations, Black Squadron," the disembodied voice said. "One million points, awarded."

The two OMBIs pulsed with the increase of strength they

had earned for passing the test, splitting the enormous value between the two.

"Yeah!" Anataur boomed excitedly.

"Level one hundred," the voice said.

All four jaws dropped.

"Get in," Anataur said as he manifested another AX-11. "We're almost through. The edge is near and I think the coastline below us is one of our OMBIcademy's training rooms."

They began to drive again through bumpy streets, going fast toward the edge. The sky above them seemed to rip open, revealing a purplish crack. Anataur focused straight ahead as the other three watched a swarm of large, red, bat-winged creatures pour out of the tear.

Looking in his mirror, Anataur yelled out, "Is that a demon swarm?"

"Yeah, looks that way!" Artemis yelled back.

"Do you think we can take it?" Anataur laughed.

"Maybe with the rest of our squad, or at least Mephisto and Vertigo," she replied.

"Just drive!" Marlena barked as the swarm darkened the sky above them.

Anataur didn't slow as they neared the edge of the floating city, driving right over the edge. He let the vehicle dissipate as they fell, the wind roaring against their ears.

The voice above them said something about, "Out of bounds for testing," but none of them were sure exactly what it said. Looking back, the demons had disappeared and the city in the clouds dimmed from sight, looking like any other large cloud.

The four fell for several minutes down toward the ocean below. Marlena wondered how they would survive, but took some comfort in the fact that neither Artemis nor Anataur seemed particularly worried.

They splashed into the ocean, going deep down before the

friction of the water stopped their descent. They swam back to the surface as Artemis formed a small inflatable raft from her OMBI. Grabbing the edges, the raft pulled them from the water quickly. Exhausted, they laboriously climbed onto the raft as it surfaced, looking at one another.

"The training rooms are non-lethal," Artemis explained.

"That would have been good to know when we were fighting the dragon." Ethan frowned.

She just smiled as she manifested a small motor, following the black line toward a high grassy cliff, overlooking the ocean.

—

Connor emerged after only two hours in orbit above Aeris VII. Staring far off into the distance as Omega sent Tizona home to Valhalla Island, Muriel showed Connor the progress of the invading fleet.

"Well, they are still pretty far, but I don't want to wait. I kind of want to see my mom's house and my room, but I guess I should wait until she's there," Connor lamented.

"Well, let's go," Connor said, opening another slipstream to the approximate location of the invasion fleet.

CHAPTER 11

The Voice of God

THE LIFT DESCENDED SLOWLY INTO A COLD METALLIC tunnel, only illuminated by a faint light above them. When they got near the bottom of the OMBIcademy, the room opened up before them into a large open space that was nearly four-hundred feet long and about one-hundred feet wide. The lift halted near the back wall, leaving William and Major Sanders far from the person on the other end.

A white-haired figure stood upon a raised dais, staring at a huge, murky glass tank, facing away from the approaching men. He was singing softly, touching the glass with one hand.

"Are you Daniel Asher?" William asked as he walked up the stairs of the dais, his gun drawn and pointed in front of him.

The man stopped singing and turned around. His white hair hung unkempt down to his shoulders. His face was young, almost childlike, with icy blue eyes that watched William and Major Sanders closely. He wore a black, one-piece flight suit and a black cape, which was draped over his right shoulder and hung down his side, to the floor.

"I am indeed the voice of God. Who are you and why have you come here?" Asher asked, his voice childish.

"I am William Mercer and I have come to ask you to surrender this ship and stop the invasion of Aeris VII. My family and

I want to go in peace; we don't want anyone else to die," he said while lowering his gun slightly to show his sincerity.

Major Sanders lowered his gun as well as the white-haired boy in front of them raised his left hand to his chin.

"I see," Asher began. "You want God to bow to mortals, is that it?"

"I recognize no God that enslaves men against their will, whether using mind control, force, or economic slavery. You come as an invader and employ all of these techniques," William stated firmly.

"But your people were created to be a slave race. You were bowing to the blood of kings, bowing to entertainment personalities and athletes, bowing to politicians and dying over arbitrary geo-political borders long before you had the technology for Him to influence you. Are you so xenophobic that when one, not of your race, does the exact thing you've been doing for centuries, that it suddenly becomes evil?" Asher reasoned.

"He makes a good point," Major Sanders said, lowering his rifle, "At least He offers immortality and power to those who follow him."

William eyed his companion with surprise.

"Resist it, Sanders," he said, turning back toward the white-haired boy.

"You error in your assumption, xenophobia is not the premise of my claim. It did not suddenly become evil to manipulate men for one's own power. It was always evil and men like me have always fought against it, either by words or by action. Our rebellious nature far exceeds our propensity to be ruled. From the earliest stories of man, we have defied the gods and devils alike, as Prometheus stole fire, Eve ate of the tree of knowledge of good and evil, as Dante faced the Inferno. So I face you." William's dark eyes narrowed as he finished.

"Ah, but you are the anomaly of your race, as were the kings before you, the few aberrations who would not be led, just like Him."

"There is a world of men standing against the UEDF, outside even as we speak! Look upon them yourself and see their defiance," William answered defiantly.

"Don't you see? They follow you, Dragoon! But still they must be led. Soon they will follow me. Look upon your entire race and I will show you, not free men, but cattle, being led to the slaughter!"

As he spoke, Asher waved his hand and the walls of the large room dissipated on one end, revealing fighters swarming around the ship and an ocean passing by below.

"Look out there and I will show you defiance even greater than my own." William grinned. "Now, Alex!"

Before Asher could react, Skoll quickly navigated the opening and flew into the room followed by Fenris, landing at the bottom of the dais, both pointing large weapons at Asher.

"It's over, Asher, surrender!" William declared.

Asher looked at the man, smiling, a glint of respect in his eyes.

"Well played," he congratulated after a moment, "but I don't think I will surrender just yet."

Asher flung his cape back, revealing a shining silver bracer upon his right hand. Silver armor formed around his body as he took a step forward.

"I'll tell you something interesting before I show you the power of the Voice of God. I was human before God gave me this," he said, holding his OMBI high. "I was the first human to wear it. Let us see what these two can do with theirs."

"William, something is keeping me from using Skoll! I'm coming out," Alex said, exiting his ship.

Austin followed, both raising their black armor as they hit

the ground. William moved first however, stepping forward to attack Asher but finding his body frozen in place.

"That's very nice armor; mechanized, isn't it?" Asher teased.

"Damn you," William growled through gritted teeth.

Standing as a statue, William watched the two soldiers from Black Squadron square off with the strange kid who wore an uninhibited OMBI.

———

The four had emerged into the OMBIcademy near Yellow Army's barracks to find it in complete disarray. They didn't waste any time, Anataur and Artemis leading Marlena and Ethan to the lift, knocking down the three men who stood in their way with one swing of Anataur's hammer.

They were heading for the observation deck and the elevator beyond. If William and Alex were in trouble as Connor said, they would be in the ship's core, like where they had fought the Xudok on Dytopa II.

The lift went up at its slow pace, impatient Marlena tapping her foot irritably the entire ride.

Upon reaching the observation deck, the four burst into the room to find Colonel Setzer unconscious on the ground. The tube was open behind the desk, the secret panel having been removed. They followed the path of those who went before them, down the tube. Through the cold metal tunnel, they descended into the darkness below. They soon emerged in the large room that now had one wall missing with ships swirling in defensive patterns beyond. The scene below was stranger still, two large battle suit vessels flanking a dais with a large murky tank and the clash of metal on metal ringing out.

Alex slid back and forth in measured strikes and retreats, light on his feet, his twin black scimitars whirling in his hands.

He moved with the elegance of a dancer in a carefully choreographed scene displaying power and control. His light blades bounced repeatedly off the silver-armored figure's glittering, two-handed great sword, which glittered as it swung back into Alex's blocking weapons, causing him to spin back a few steps before charging back in.

Austin moved opposite Alex, flanking the silver knight, his black sword and shield coming in quickly at his opponent's back before being turned away with a heavy swing. The figure in silver moved quickly, wielding the sword as if it were weightless. On the dais, a stunned William Mercer and a contemplative Major Sanders watched the fight unfolding too.

Asher's quick steps forced Alex and Austin back on their heels and it became apparent that neither were a match for the armored boy alone. Together they could barely hold the boy to a standstill, but as Anataur's roar pierced the battlefield, Alex was grinning.

Several arrows flew in above them, which Asher picked off quickly with his sword, taking a few steps back and studying the new combatants.

Anataur moved between Alex and Austin, nodding to his old comrades as Artemis took up a position on Skoll's now kneeling form, surveying the battlefield.

Marlena ran around the battle, using her enhanced speed to try to get to William. Asher caught sight of her, and, smiling, locked her battle armor in place inches away from her husband.

Through it all Ethan stood back, watching Alex, amazed at the strong man that his son had become. In that moment, more than any of the last few days with Connor and Marlena, Ethan felt a sense of profound regret at his decision to leave.

"Well, this is an interesting surprise. The Phoenix has been reborn and her son's friends have come to play," Asher taunted.

Asher moved quickly, charging forward and deflecting

another arrow that came from above with his large sword. He swung his blade in a hard arc toward Anataur with such speed that Anataur barely got his heavy hammer up in time to block. Asher followed the move with a quick kick, which knocked the broad-shouldered boy off the steps and onto the ground below.

Arrows rained in from above as Alex and Austin moved back into the fight, attacking furiously, using the arrow blocks to find openings in Asher's defenses. Alex scored two quick hits, before dodging back out of the reach of the large sword, an arrow marking a third hit as Asher moved to block Austin's attack from the other side.

Asher's armor was strong though, and the boy didn't seem to tire. Coming back in hard against Austin's shield, he slammed it until the boy's arm went numb. The move cost him two more arrow hits, which bit deeply into his armor.

Back on his feet, Anataur joined the ranks and the three melee fighters of Black Squadron surrounded their foe, dancing forward and back, dishing out minor hits while Artemis kept a steady stream of distracting arrows raining down.

Even with his enhanced speed and uninhibited OMBI, Asher was hard pressed. One weapon became two as he fought with two great swords before one extended into a bladed whip, coming around and hitting Austin in the back, causing his armor to weaken. Not to be outdone, Austin let his sword become a long spear, which he used to stab Asher every time he moved to block one of Alex's or Anataur's strikes.

The dance continued for several minutes, Asher taking ten hits for every one he delivered. The battle took a turn when Anataur managed to clip Asher's leg, sending him spinning to the ground from the heavy blow. Alex and Austin were on him in a second, the ringing of metal on metal sounding like one continuous note as Alex's blades whirled against Asher's armor.

The silver-armored boy managed to get up, spinning and

swinging out two bladed whips, until he found his feet. The armor on his right arm had dissipated and, finally seeing results of their ongoing attack, the four members of black squadron pressed on.

Austin's armor had diminished in several places by then and he was bleeding from several small cuts. Anataur had lost his helmet and in the next move Asher unleashed a cunning attack that deeply cut the large boy's left eye. Anataur roared in pain, blood spewing from the wound as he swung his hammer wildly, making Asher pay for the damage.

During the wild attack, Asher's guard dropped and an arrow bit hard into his shoulder. He recoiled in pain and, using the distraction, Alex was on him in a flash. His swords rattled against the other boy's head in rapid succession, knocking him back and dispelling his helmet.

The fight stopped the second Alex knocked Asher's riposte up high and his second blade stopped against Asher's neck.

"Well fought," Alex said, breathing heavily.

Asher's smile unnerved Alex as he stepped back away from the blade. Alex pressed his arm forward to finish Asher off, but found that he couldn't move. His blade still out, Alex struggled.

"That's enough of that. It was a good fight, but one you could never win." Asher smirked, inspecting Anataur's blood on his silver blade.

"What did you do to us?" Alex growled through clenched teeth.

"God has taken control of the entire 1st fleet and every ship between here and the Orbital Defense Grid control center. He can stop a few of your OMBI. Those inhibitor chips make you easy to control," Asher teased as he stepped in front of Alex.

"This must be hard on your mother, watching her oldest son die. Do you have any last words?" Asher smiled.

Asher's blade shot forward and met flesh too quickly. He hadn't noticed the form of the tall man who had moved to block the strike, but as his long blade pierced Ethan Pereira's abdomen, Asher let out a delighted laugh.

"Ah, thus the father redeems himself in the selfless act of sacrifice for his son, marvelous! Futile, but touching nonetheless," Asher chirped.

"Dad!?" Alex cried, seeing the man in the room for the first time.

"Alex, I'm sorry," Ethan sputtered as he coughed a lungful of blood.

Alex growled with rage. Asher peeked over Ethan's shoulder, looking at Alex as he pushed his sword farther through Ethan's stomach, causing the man to groan in pain.

Despite the fatal blow, Ethan smirked, just before he grabbed the neck of white-haired kid and pulled him back with all his strength into Alex's stationary blade.

The blade punctured Asher's eye and his great sword dissipated, dropping Ethan to the floor.

"No!" Major Sanders yelled, moving for the first time since the fight began. He ran to Asher's side, sobbing. As the others felt their bonds release, Sanders picked up the boy and carried him up the dais, wailing.

Alex immediately dropped to his knees and inspected Ethan's wound. He knew there were no AFMR nearby to help him, and he watched the light fading from his father's eyes.

"I'm sorry, Alex. I should have been there, through all of it," Ethan whispered, blood dripping from his lips. "I always meant to come back, but one day I blinked and years had gone by. I'm a fool."

"It's okay, Dad. I forgive you for that. You were there when it mattered. You saved my life," Alex said as tears formed in his eyes.

Marlena was by her son's side as they watched the light fade out of Ethan's eyes. Artemis, Anataur, and Austin all stood by, watching the scene unfold, as did William Mercer, feeling great sympathy and understanding for the man who had sacrificed himself for his son.

William's grief didn't hold him though, as his eyes met his wife's for the first time in six years. They walked slowly toward each other, unsure of what to say after the years and given such dark circumstances. Marlena had tears in her almond eyes, overwhelmed by the weight of the moment.

When they stood face to face, there was too much to say to put into words. They had both mourned the other in their time and fought for the same values in the memory of each other. The distance and time between them tore them both apart, but in that moment they both felt as if they had never left each other's side.

William put his arms around his wife and pulled her close. They held each other tight, as if they had never intended to let go.

Even Alex smiled, despite the weight on his heart, knowing how long William and Marlena had been waiting to see each other.

Major Sanders set Asher's body at the base of the murky-watered tank and knelt as if praying. No one paid him much heed, all lost in their respective moments.

"The ships," Austin began. "The enemy ships are still flying."

Alex was on his feet in an instant, looking out the opened wall at the strange swarming pattern of the unpiloted ships.

"It isn't over," William remarked, turning toward Major Sanders. "What's in the tank, Sanders?"

Sanders turned toward them smiling.

"How can you not see? We are here to witness the birth of a new world. Humanity is a disease upon the galaxy that must be purged. How many Adolph Hitlers, Joseph Stalins, or General Harruhamas will we endure? How many Franklin Setzers plot against our children or Philip Wicks prey upon the weak? We are a sick race. We have depleted this planet and now infest dozens more, all of it with our mouths open and our hands out. We must stand against them, to defy those who loot the work of the producers. What kind of world are we leaving to our children?" Sanders declared with his arms above his head.

"Interesting, whatever is controlling him preys upon the beliefs and values of the one it's trying to control. There is no reasoning with a creature that only believes in destruction and coercion," William commented, raising his shotgun.

"Wait!" Sanders pleaded, causing William to hesitate. "Phoenix, if we don't stop the people who put the EMC in power, then we can't stop the invasion fleet. What if Aeris is destroyed? Where in the universe will be safe for your children? Where can you finally be with William in peace?"

"Mephisto," he continued, "will your brother ever be safe with a warmonger race fighting its own people for resources? Would you condemn him to the same life you are destined to face? The constant fight to protect the ones you love? Shouldn't he know peace?"

"Steel your minds, do not let it find a way in," William said, trying to resist the waves of control.

He tried to pull the trigger, but couldn't find the strength, wondering what a world without beggars would be like. He felt Marlena's hand upon his, her warm touch sending chills down his spine. She took his three-barreled shotgun from his hands and looked him in the eye with a soft smile.

"You've carried this for so long, let me carry it the rest of the way."

She aimed high, unloading both barrels of explosive pellets into the side of the murky tank. A large crack appeared, sending dark-green liquid spraying outward. As the crack grew, Alex and Anataur joined Artemis on Skoll, while William, Marlena, and Austin begun to climb Fenris.

Even Sanders had the self-preservation instincts to jump to

the side as the glass burst, flooding the large room in a wave of green murky water that spilled out the open wall on the far side.

At the top of the dais, a large yellow blob pulsed from the remains of the tank. The mass grew outward slowly, taking form. It rippled and pulsed, reaching thirty feet high, and opened a large eye, which quickly moved around, looking at everyone in the room individually.

"Xudok," Marlena whispered breathlessly.

Unlike the Xudok on Dytopa II, this one was not chained up, nor was it wounded. It was also much bigger than the one they had encountered the day before.

Sitting on Fenris' shoulder, Marlena grabbed a shell from William's cartridge belt and loaded it in the weapon, firing at the eye as soon as the barrel clicked into place.

The explosive pellets detonated just short of the Xudok's massive eye, causing a ripple of colors to shimmer as the shield absorbed the impact.

"It has an OMBI!" Artemis called out, firing several arrows into the shield. "It must be how it's controlling these ships!"

Major Sanders stood up and began laughing, moving beside the monstrous blob.

"You petty things," he spoke, but it was not the voice of Major Sanders coming from his mouth, but a deeper, richer voice. "It is so much worse than you think."

The Xudok's tentacles began to emerge from its body, ten appendages full of a strange, dark liquid, pulsing as they grew longer. They saw their doom in that moment; upon each of the tentacles was a silver shining OMBI.

CHAPTER 12

The Xudok King

C ONNOR EMERGED FROM HIS SLIPSTREAM IN AN EMPTY part of space; the stars glittered brightly in the endless night around him. For a moment the boy just sat and stared, letting the knowledge of his ship and sentient bracers fill his mind. He recognized so many places that he began to wonder if Muriel, Omega, and Hati had been everywhere in the universe.

"No," Muriel answered from Connor's silver shining OMBI, "our collective conscious has been far but we are beings far younger than the universe, and even now it expands into new places."

Connor tried to wrap his mind around the idea of things coming into existence from a universe of finite energy.

"Like we manifest your will when you call, so the universe manifests too," the feminine voice explained in his mind.

"Whose will is the universe manifesting?" Connor whispered aloud.

"We still search for the answer to that question," she said.

"Well, where did you come from?" Connor asked.

In response, Connor's mind filled with images of a lush planet in a binary star system that he didn't recognize. The image shifted to a floating city full of technology that Connor knew his mind wasn't ready to understand. Translucent beings floated about purposefully with glittering silver arm bands on their wrists.

"Our race was born and flourished relatively shortly after time began to flow linearly. We were an inquisitive species and set out to explore the galaxy. We were so eager to make contact with other races that when we had discovered the Xudoks, we welcomed them among us. It wasn't long before they began to attempt to dominate our people. The only way we could protect our minds was to eliminate our biological elements and become the bracers we wore. We protected our brothers and sisters as symbiotic technological devices, fighting back and nearly destroying the Xudoks. We captured their leaders and, not wanting to be responsible for genocide, we sent them into far corners of the galaxy. It has been a long time since there has been a biological Cryptolith; we exist now in this form, hoping to serve a worthy initiator, like you."

Connor listened, captivated.

"That is why they inhibited the OMBI, so we wouldn't know any of this. But why did they give us OMBI at all?" Connor asked.

"T'orath, the Xudok king on Earth, needed help from humans to break free of his bindings. He enslaved the mind of the first human to discover his signal and made his goal to enslave your race, giving you many of our technologies like slipstreams and OMBI devices in order to coax you into exploration, to find other Xudoks. As powerful as T'orath is, he cannot enslave all of your people without help," Omega explained in his ten-year-old voice.

"Why? What is the purpose of enslaving a race?" Connor asked, understanding suddenly why William had always questioned the ultimate motivations of everyone.

"Power. Xudoks don't age but they also don't reproduce. We believe that they were created in the first moments of the expansion of the universe. Mortal species exist to propagate within their environment, immortal species exist to fulfill a different purpose. It is a Xudok's nature to dominate in the same way it was the Cryptolith's purpose to explore and gather knowledge. In a sense, they are the same," Muriel answered.

"How is that the same?" Connor's face scrunched in confusion.

"We all seek to be the still point in an expanding universe. As far as we can conceive existence, so it grows. As we understand, so we empower ourselves in our space and time. A Xudok does the same thing by controlling a race through force. We both accept our role as we have been cast, unlike you, who defy the role you have been given. You are different, even among your species, which is why you were able to work around the inhibitors."

"What makes me different?" Connor asked, wide-eyed.

"We do not know," Muriel said cryptically.

"Well that was a waste of time." Connor pouted, turning his attention back to the task he had set himself upon.

He could feel that the invasion fleet was close and let himself slip into the slower slipstream space at an even pace with the frigates around him.

The frigates appeared in the space around him, speeding toward Aeris VII. Shutting his eyes, Connor reached out through his OMBI into each of the eighty-six ships around him. In his mind, Connor was throwing a lariat around them over and over again. It was not a simple task to remember the name and slip-drive code for each of them, but Connor allowed his mind to clear and refused to give up.

Once he had them all, he grabbed the rope in his mind and pulled back as hard as he could.

The ships immediately slowed, being forced back into normal space. They held their positions for a moment before turning on the small battle suit vessel while arming their weapons.

Connor could feel the powerful cannons in each ship lock on to him as he focused.

The communicator in Hati lit up and the commander of the 2nd fleet appeared on the small screen.

"UEDF Hati, stand down! Surrender and prepare to be taken aboard," the commander ordered.

"Commander Ragnar of the 2nd fleet, my name is Connor Pereira and I have pulled you out of your slipstream because what you're doing is wrong. Your enemy is not the Independent Colonies but a creature that has been manipulating the leaders of the UEDF," the boy said honestly, appealing to the man's sense of morality.

There was a moment of silence before Commander Ragnar replied, "Do you have any evidence of your claim?"

In response, Connor opened a slipstream to Earth, pulling data through his OMBI, focusing on the events unfolding around the OMBIcademy. He wasn't sure how he was aware of what was happening, but he could feel the connection between Hati and Skoll as if they were somehow always aware of each other, even on opposite sides of the galaxy. Focusing, Connor transmitted the data to all the frigates.

The feed continued for several minutes, the image of the OMBIcademy lifting into the air and the audio transmissions of the crew of the frigates of the 1st fleet being controlled by something.

"Will you help me save humanity?" Connor asked simply.

Commander Ragnar didn't answer right away, but several of the other commanders did.

"Yes, sir," they replied, until Ragnar also replied.

"Okay, let's go do it then," Connor smiled.

He turned with the entirety of the 2nd, 6th, 7th, and 8th fleets at his back. Connor opened a huge slipstream, pulling toward

Earth as hard as he could, sending all the ships in before following them.

———

With a nod from Alex, Anataur charged the bulbous creature, yelling as he ran up the stairs, swinging his massive hammer as hard as he could. The hammer collided against silver armor that formed over the huge creature. Anataur didn't let up, swinging over and over at the same spot.

Artemis jumped down from Skoll and knelt down, aiming for the eye of the beast, changing the type of arrow she fired with each shot, hoping to find a weakness. Incendiary arrows caused a reddish ripple against the shield, ice arrows caused a silvery blue splatter, lightning bolts flashed against a yellow barrier. Artemis even formed her ballista and launched larger bolts at the unconcerned Xudok.

Alex and Austin used the distraction to board their battle suit vessels and manifesting large swords, then began to attack the beast. Armor deflected the first few hits, but soon a variety of silvery weapons began to appear in the ten tentacles, blocking and returning strikes against the more powerful foes.

A gigantic sword blocked Alex's scimitars as a trident poked out from the side, crashing into his armor, followed by a hammer strike from above. Skoll slammed into the ground hard, stunning Alex slightly. Fenris was above him immediately, fending off attacks from ten tentacle appendages with a shield and sword.

Alex didn't waste the reprieve and was up in an instant, moving to the side, attacking one tentacle as it shot past him with a large spear. The armored appendage didn't give at all as Alex struck it. It did, however, reverse its direction, slamming into Skoll, knocking Alex back against the wall.

Fenris took several hits that Austin was unable to block,

each strike weakening his armor significantly until it began to fail in several places. Unable to go on the offensive, Austin focused on dodging and blocking attacks that he couldn't keep up with, rapid strikes chipping away at his defenses.

William hadn't been idle during the fight, but was not immediately effective against the massive, bulbous creature. His explosive pellets rippled off the thing's shield, followed by a stream of thermite discs, which caused the shield to glow bright red. The armored eye of the Xudok looked right at him as he fired and swung a large tentacle at him, knocking him to the ground across the room.

Marlena fired a few shots from her sidearm, but realized quickly that she wouldn't be able to be much help with such a small weapon, and instead charged and attacked Major Sanders, who seemed surprised as Marlena slammed him with her shoulder. The Major, dazed, was easily overcome by the strength of Marlena's mechanized battle armor. She took the unconscious man's auto rifle and ran back to where William was getting up, firing controlled bursts that rippled across the shield.

Anataur was the first to go down, being knocked back hard as the entire Xudok shifted forward as it attacked Skoll. His head struck the ground hard, causing him to lose consciousness.

Austin was next. Unable to keep his armor up, taking damage directly to Fenris, he had to abandon his ship as it took a hit from two axes that crushed its torso. The hulking ship knelt down and fell over as Austin rolled out of the cockpit, sword in hand. The Xudok wasn't done with him however, dissipating one of its weapons and pushing him up against a wall, covering him with a slimy residue, which hardened quickly, trapping the boy.

Artemis continued her barrage as the Xudok began to spit chunks of goo toward her from a large beak that appeared below its eye. She dove and rolled to avoid the goo. The ground grew saturated and her foot got stuck in one of the pools. She stopped dodging and continued to fire arrows as fast as he could until the goo crawled up her leg and solidified around her arm as well. Her bow became a pistol in one hand, which she kept attacking with, refusing to give up when a second stream of slime covered and solidified over her entire body, leaving only her head uncovered.

Down to three foes, the Xudok concentrated more on its attacks. One tentacle moved quickly, grabbing William's dangerous shotgun and flinging it out the large opening on the opposite side of the ship. The same tentacle came back and took Marlena's auto rifle, leaving both of them unarmed and unable to help Alex, who now was backed into a corner against the full attack of ten armed appendages.

To his credit, Alex spun and moved Skoll ahead of nearly all the attacks, dodging and rolling around behind the Xudok, where none of his family or friends were vulnerable on the ground. Not having to worry about accidentally stepping on someone, Alex moved much quicker, Skoll's twin scimitars rattling off armored goo in between deflecting swings.

The fight continued for several minutes, Alex moving like a man possessed, knowing that he could not fall less he doom all of humanity. He carried the weight of the responsibility like a champion, modifying his weapons between attacks, countering every attack thrown at him.

The Xudok huffed in frustration as the smaller battle suit danced and spun ahead of its most cunning attacks. The armor generated from ten different uninhibited OMBIs remained undamaged though, and T'orath knew that it was only a matter of time before the human made a mistake. As it was, Alex didn't make so much of a mistake, as he wasn't completely aware of all of the Xudok's abilities. The thing let its weapons dissipate and spread its tentacles out wide, rushing forward into Skoll, slamming him into the wall. As the Xudok backed up back to the dais,

Alex found that Skoll was affixed to the wall by the same strange, hard goo that encased the other members of Black Squadron.

They all felt the Xudok as it tried to get into their minds, every thought being tilted toward its will. The only defense seemed to be to try not to think at all. Without action to fuel their fight, they moved into an internal struggle, trying to resist domination.

Soon Major Sanders was on his feet again, walking unsteadily back to the side of the creature.

"T'orath congratulates you on your well-fought battle. You are the strong, defiant few, who had the courage to stand for your values. Once you accept Him as your God, you will serve well by his side," Sanders bellowed, raising his arms in the air.

"Oh, joy," William said to Marlena.

"First things first, though. Bear witness, heroes of humanity, to the end of your rebellion."

Ahead, in the Mountains of Colorado, several thousand free men and former UEDF troops gathered armed with military equipment and vehicles.

From the opening in the wall, they watched as atmospheric fighters flew in tight formations, firing immediately upon the unmanned swarms of RA fighters. The OMBIcademy slowed as the 1st fleet and its escort of thousands of unmanned fighters, acquired in the flight from Kita-Daito, moved forward to engage the last resistance of mankind.

To their credit, the defenders of the Orbital Defense Grid control center were well entrenched for battle and put up a good fight. Though extremely outnumbered and outgunned, they fought valiantly. Anti-aircraft guns knocked hundreds of fighters from the sky before frigate cannons destroyed them. Though the frigates took little damage themselves, men from the ground, armed with shoulder-mounted launchers, fired upwards by the dozens, small rockets slamming into large ships in tiny puffs of smoke and debris.

One frigate went down, its core falling out of the center unceremoniously.

"The crew must have ejected it themselves," William explained to Marlena as they watched the large ship smash into the ground.

The man and his wife held hands, unable to do anything against the mighty Xudok; they could only watch the battle unfold below them.

They had tried to go up the tube back to the observation room to find reinforcements from within the OMBIcademy, but the lift was gone and didn't return.

"Isn't there anything we can do?" Marlena asked her husband as she leaned against him.

"I really don't know," William answered honestly, looking at the ground.

The battle below continued on. After almost an hour of fighting, the defenders got some unexpected reinforcements as dozens of large transports landed, full of former UEDF troops and free men. They charged forward into the horribly one-sided fight, firing their weapons into the swarming squadrons of unmanned fighters.

The Xudok held very still, its large eye staring out at the battle. Even Major Sanders was quiet. The tentacles flailed slightly as fighters went down and ships moved.

"I think it's concentrating on the battle. Amazing it can control so many things at once," William commented.

"If we only had something to attack it with right now," Marlena growled, looking around for any weapon.

She still had her side arm that only had five bullets left. She held it and looked at the armored Xudok doubtfully. Before she got the chance to decide whether or not to risk the attack, the OMBIcademy lurched forward, moving toward the Orbital Defense Grid control center. Cheyenne Mountain loomed ahead; upon it sat several large dishes, which pointed at various directions in the sky.

The OMBIcademy came to a stop over the summit and lowered so it was nearly touching the top of it. From the bottom of the ship, long cables stretched downward through the earth, digging downward. Nothing happened for a few moments, but soon the Xudok opened its large eye, its iris fluttering as the power of its OMBIs overwhelmed the grid's AI.

"Witness the end," Major Sanders said in the eerie deep voice.

He raised his arm and pointed as a beam of light enveloped a squadron of defending ships that had managed to avoid destruction thus far.

The light brightened painfully and then disappeared. The ships exploded in midair, the ground below them bursting apart, launching huge chunks of rock and dirt.

As if testing the orbital defense grid, the Xudok forced a long line of energy out, which cascaded like a wave of light over the plains beyond, erupting into a tremendous explosion, which shook the entire ship, almost knocking William and Marlena to the ground.

"No…" the raven-haired woman whispered, a tear in her eye forming as the sheer devastation of Earth's defense grid turned against the planet it was meant to protect.

The OMBIcademy rose upward, no threat of being attacked by the grid now; the Xudok lifted it and the fleet it controlled high into the sky. Though smaller after the battle, the swarm of fighters continued to wrap itself in strange patterns around the OMBIcademy. Seeing farther at that height, the Xudok moved the ship forward, beams of light tearing through the cloudless sky down, striking the Earth below. The creature didn't seem to discriminate on what targets to attack, destroying everything it could see.

The attack was interrupted momentarily when one of the frigate crews managed to override the onboard AI and take control of a cannon, which it fired at the OMBIcademy ship. The blast caused the ship to shake violently, but did little damage against the strong Cryptolith metal.

In response, the Xudok looked sideways, turning toward the frigate, which it engulfed with a beam of light, destroying it entirely.

Devastation rained upon the Earth as the ship flew across North America, the defense grid responding to the will of the terrible beast controlling it.

—

From Earth's moon, the residents of the Lunar Colony stood looking up at the Earth as it lit up over and over like a great storm moving across the face of the planet. They had heard the Earth was under attack before the communications had ceased. Some were crying from inside the large dome, others were trying desperately to contact their family on the planet.

They were still watching when the space between the Earth and the Moon distorted and several large figures emerged from the slipstream. Cheers went up when they recognized the frigates of the 2nd, 6th, 7th, and 8th UEDF fleets returning to Earth.

—

Hati came through last, but quickly moved to the head of the column of warships, taking in the scene ahead of them.

"… and today I save Earth." Connor smirked to himself, trying to imagine the outcome he desired most to see.

Connor opened a communication line to the commanders of the four fleets behind him.

"Okay, 7th and 8th fleets, that Orbital Defense Grid is attacking Earth, launch your fighters and take out as much of it as you can," Connor ordered.

"Roger," the commanders replied simultaneously.

"6th fleet, punch a hole through and attack the grid control center. The sooner you disable it, the fewer people will die."

"Yes, sir," the 6th fleet commander responded, his ships moving ahead of the column.

"2nd fleet, stay with me as best you can. We need to find the thing responsible for this."

"Yes sir," Commander Ragnar responded.

Connor shut his eyes and took a deep breath.

"Okay, Omega, Hati, and Muriel, let's go!" Connor said, opening his eyes.

He activated the Locate function on his OMBI, which drew a blue line down toward North America, toward his brother. Connor urged Hati forward toward the grid, as the seven wings of the wolf-faced ship separated and formed into large beam cannons, which orbited around him.

Connor moved his ship forward faster, his cannons spinning around his ship, firing long beams of energy into the defense grid ahead, spreading outward as they fired, punching a hole though the grid large enough for him and the 2nd fleet to get through. The Defense Grid immediately ceased firing on Earth and turned toward the returning fleets, firing cannons at the frigates.

Fighters launched from the two fleets staying in orbit and the frigates returned fire as many of them took hits, causing a cascade of explosions on both the grid and the fleets. The fighters dodged more effectively and moved closer to use their smaller weapons, firing on the small weapon arrays that made up the grid.

The 2nd fleet took a fair bit of damage moving through. The

ships that were heavily damaged launched their fighters to protect the other ships in the fleet as well as they could as the 2nd fleet, led by the white battle suit vessel, pierced the atmosphere and flew straight down into the waiting 1st fleet.

—

"Aim to disable, not to kill. They are being controlled by something," Connor ordered Commander Ragnar.

The cannons of both fleets fired upon each other. The ships that missed from the 2nd fleet rained destruction upon the plains of South Dakota, spraying rock high into the air. Through the explosions, Connor spun and dodged around the heavy, slow cannon fire.

Spotting his target, Connor flew toward the OMBIcademy, dodging wildly. Keeping his focus on the battle, Connor watched, mesmerized by the intricate patterns of the swarms of unmanned fighters moving to protect the facility from attack. Hati's spinning beam cannons fired into the swarm, causing hundreds of explosions, destroying large swaths of swarming ships.

One beam went through the enemy ships and slammed into the side of the OMBIcademy, leaving the silvery metal scorched and blackened, but undamaged. Connor let Hati aim and fire his cannons at will, manifesting homing rockets on his legs and arms and two rail machine guns in his hands.

The rockets burst outward, whirling through the air, tracking nearby targets and destroying them. Connor turned his railguns into a deadly stream of magnetically propelled projectiles that tore through dozens of ships per shot as the swarm quickly crumbled before the uninhibited might of Hati.

Hati turned during the fight to fire beams back up into the 1st fleet, which was now fully engaged with the 2nd fleet. The beams ripped into the hull, disabling some of the large cannons.

The remains of the swarm changed tactics and began flying directly at Connor, detonating when they got near. Connor began to sweat from the effort of keeping his shield's up. Diving Hati straight downward, then swinging up toward the base of the OMBIcademy, Connor flew straight into the large room over William and Marlena and landed in front of T'orath.

T'orath rose quickly from its position, stretching tall and reaching its tentacles toward Hati. Connor didn't wait, but charged straight in, using his powerful fists to pound away at the armor of the large creature.

The tentacles wrapped around the battle suit, pulling it close, fighting against Connor's strength and squeezing Hati's arms and legs together, wrapping itself close. Connor drove Hati's head right into the eye of the beast and shut his eyes.

Connor's will was strong and the entities in his OMBIs reached out for T'orath's OMBIs while they were locked together.

—

The room changed to William and Marlena, taking on the form of a broken planet in the light of a red sun. The one missing wall, still a window to the war on Earth, made the scene disorienting. In the middle of the room, Connor stood beside a tall woman in a shimmering silver dress and a young boy who looked like William Mercer as a child. They faced off against the Xudok and ten silver knights, all wearing armor and holding shining long swords. Major Sanders took a step out of the way, standing off to the side, watching eagerly.

Anataur and Artemis watched from the side, their unmoving forms struggling to take part in the battle. Austin sat staring from the wall, which in the landscape appeared as a large rock. Skoll took the form of a small dragon, which Alex was sitting on top of. Both were affixed by chains to a rock on the far side of the standoff.

"What is this?" Marlena asked.

"The core of this ship is capable of manifesting like a training room," Omega answered, not taking his eyes off the enemies in front of him.

"But what are we seeing?" William demanded breathlessly.

"A manifestation of the combination of the minds of Connor and T'orath," Omega answered.

T'orath moved forward, holding weapons in each of its ten flailing tentacles.

"You cannot win a battle of wills against me, boy!" the one-eyed creature barked from its large beak.

"He is powerful here, move quickly," Muriel cautioned, looking down at Connor. "Those Cryptoliths have had their souls drained and now serve T'orath."

"Is that why they're faceless?" Connor asked, frowning.

"Yes," came the deep growl from behind Connor.

The large wolf manifested behind the boy, snarling at the faceless knights.

"Hati!" Connor chirped, smiling.

"Focus, initiator," the wolf growled in its low voice.

A cool wind blew across the desolate landscape then. All at once, both groups moved toward each other.

Connor leapt over the soulless knights right at T'orath, using his bare hands to block a pair of swords that were swung at him, easily deflecting them away. Connor returned the attack by punching up into the tentacles that were closest, causing the beast to shuffle away.

Omega faced off against a pair of knights, manifesting his own armor and sword, picking off the attacks neatly and returning the attacks systematically like they belonged in a choreographed scene in a play, neither side gaining ground.

Muriel moved against three knights quickly, flipping around them with a long knife in each hand, which she jabbed forward and blocked with, causing pinholes to appear in the enemy knight's armor, strange silver blood oozing from the wounds.

Hati moved even quicker, leaping into the middle of the remaining five knights, grabbing one his mighty jaws and shaking it violently before throwing it down onto the ground. The aggressive assault cost the great wolf a few stinging cuts, which it seemed to ignore as it thrashed and howled at the remaining four.

From where William was watching he could see Skoll trying desperately to break free from the wall each time Hati yelped. Alex struggled against his chains too, watching Connor fight a huge opponent alone.

"Left, Tons!" Alex called out, warning Connor of an income strike.

"Thanks, Alex," Connor shot back, dodging out of the way.

Connor circled T'orath, when the thing hit him on the side with a large hammer. Connor accepted the hit and rolled with it, slamming into the wall just below where Alex was suspended.

"Thank you, idiot," Connor quipped as he hopped up, leaping upward toward his brother.

Gripping the chain with both hands, he yanked as hard as he could.

—

Outside the OMBIcademy ship, Commander Ragnar was hard pressed against the 1st fleet until Connor flew inside the great ship. After a few moments, the swarms of fighters began colliding and communications started coming in from various frigates of the 1st fleet that they had regained control. Both fleets were heavily damaged, but as the fight in the ship below continued, fewer and fewer of the frigates from the 1st fleet were attacking until they had all levelled off and began to set down in the plains of South Dakota, their damage keeping them from continuing to battle.

Farther up from the battle around the OMBIcademy, the Orbital Defense Grid shut down completely as the 6th fleet disabled the control center on the ground. The battered 7th and 8th fleets, getting a reprieve, moved down through the atmosphere to assist the other damaged fleets on the ground.

—

The Xudok moved fast toward Connor, who was pulling against Alex's chains. Manifesting a 311 AFMR in his place, Connor dove back against the charging monster, hitting it several times in the eye, before rolling off to the side to avoid being skewered by a trident.

The AFMR began working quickly on Alex's bracer, while holding itself up by the chains with its third arm.

T'orath turned back toward Alex, but Connor didn't give it the time to do anything about the AFMR, attacking recklessly. He took several cuts as he refused to give ground to the larger opponent, jumping, diving, and kicking the beast with every chance he had.

Omega and Muriel were keeping up with their attackers, not giving or gaining much ground in their battles. Hati had backed into a defensive stance. Surrounded by prodding enemies, the wolf snapped and spun around, keeping his enemies at bay, until another black-armored man appeared in the battle.

"Argonaut!" Omega greeted as the black knight moved ahead with a large black sword, slamming it against one of the armored knights attacking Omega, knocking it back.

Skoll, the black-armored dragon, joined the fight with Hati against the four remaining attackers, overwhelming one of them quickly by biting it in half.

Alex joined the fight too, his OMBI now uninhibited and his eyes glowing green as he attacked T'orath with his two scimitars.

Connor and Alex stayed on opposite sides of the creature, keeping it spinning as it tried to watch both boys at once. Connor's fists were a blur as he punched hard against the creature, using its own tentacles to launch off when they got close, pounding the side of the bulbous head and leaving deep depressions in the thing's sickly yellow skin.

Alex's swords did more damage still, cutting deeply and leaving enormous gashes. As T'orath tried to hit him, Alex ducked and severed the tentacle that was swinging at him. As he did, one of the silver knights fighting Muriel disappeared. She saluted Alex with her sword and turned back to her fight, gaining ground against her enemies.

Xudok roared and spun in a quick circle, its weapons held out at various lengths and heights like a whirlwind of slicing metal. Connor jumped backwards while Alex jumped into the whirlwind, flipping as he went, dodging the weapons driving his blades into the beast's eye.

The landscape faded back into the gray room. Sanders fell to the floor, gripping his head, and T'orath's severed tentacle fell to the floor, releasing Hati.

Alex was a blur, his uninhibited OMBI giving him enormous strength as he broke free of the goo that was holding Skoll and manifested his scimitars. In a whirlwind, he attacked the back of the unarmored T'orath. The giant, thin blades bit deep into the yellow flesh, causing black ichor to pour out onto Skoll as the Xudok thrashed and flailed. Alex held it in place as well as he could as Connor and Hati moved in front of it, punching the beast's great eye.

The sound of the eye popping made everyone in the room cringe slightly as the beaked monstrosity released a piercing squeal. The flailing tentacles battered Hati and Skoll, knocking them backwards.

T'orath, now blind, started dragging itself on nine tentacles toward the open wall on the far end of the large room. It moved toward where Anataur and Artemis were stuck, and had almost crawled over them when it lurched backwards. Grabbing it by one of the tentacles, Skoll dragged the beast back and held it in place while it flailed and screamed.

"I've had enough!" Connor yelled, manifesting a long silver spear in Hati's large hands.

Connor spun the spear over his head and used Hati's thrusters to fly up then came down hard.

The spear pierced the bulbous Xudok, straight through its eye socket, biting into the ground on the dais.

"Take that, Fish Mouth!" Connor cried loudly.

Immediately the OMBIcademy began to fall out of the sky, gaining speed as it plummeted to the plains of South Dakota.

"Connor, come on!" Alex yelled, flying his ship out the large opening, dropping from sight.

Without hesitation, Connor followed his brother out of the ship and smiled as he passed by William and Marlena.

Alex took position on one side of the OMBIcademy, pressing Skoll's back against the huge ship and pushing upwards against it.

Connor took his position on the opposite side and fired his thrusters hard.

The OMBIcademy began to slow slightly.

"Give it all you got, Tons!" Alex yelled into his communicator. Skoll's eyes flashed bright green as Alex used every ounce of his willpower to prevent the ship from crashing down.

Connor had his eyes closed, lifting the impossibly heavy ship, thinking about his mom and stepdad inside, about all his friends in Blue Army who were counting on him. He knew they were slowing it down, but he wasn't sure how far he had before it crashed, so he pushed even harder.

His heart was racing in his chest, pounding against his ribs painfully. Connor opened his eyes as he felt the ground beneath his feet and realized he and Alex were holding the ship up.

"Now what?" Connor yelled to Alex.

"Let go, let's push it down now so it doesn't fall over!" Alex shouted back.

The two let go, moving swiftly to the upper levels of the ship before it tipped over. Using the same effort, they pushed downward, driving the ship into the Earth below. Once it had gone deep enough to hold its own weight they stopped, breathing heavily and sweating profusely.

Barely able to think, Connor landed on the ground, next to the great ship, and got out of his battle suit, falling to his knees.

Alex landed Skoll next to Hati and got out of the kneeling ship, collapsing on the ground next to Connor.

Both boys lay back on the dirt and looked up at the smoking ships of Earth's fleets landing around the OMBIcademy.

Connor looked at Alex, who looked back at him, smiling.

"Take that, Fish Mouth?" Alex laughed.

"I guess it sounded cooler in my head," Connor retorted, removing his shoe and throwing it Alex's way.

Alex caught the shoe and began laughing harder. His laugh was infectious and soon Connor joined in.

"Good job, kid," Alex said, smiling at his brother.

Connor turned his head back to watch the ships landing, with a smile on his face.

EPILOGUE

THE MONTHS AFTER THE END OF THE REVOLUTION and the defeat of T'orath went by in a blur. The UEDF disbanded, and the remaining fleets divided themselves among the colonies. A few elected to stay on Earth, led by a new council, consisting of the former councilman Moreau and councilwoman Morgan along with the leaders of the free man revolution. Earth had been devastated during the revolution and in the battle with the Xudok.

Many people had died in the fighting, and of the remaining population many elected to find work in the colonies. Earth was still the largest planet in terms of population, with nearly two billion people. The decreased strain on their resources helped them in the endeavor to rebuild, along with support from the colonies. Each colony elected its own leaders to represent them in trade with other colonies, everyone working toward their own success with the support of strong infrastructure and an abundance of galactic resources.

—

"Are you sure this is what he wants?" Mr. Sanders asked the dark-haired figure on the other side of the video display.

"What else could you get him, Mr. Sanders? This will only work if it's a complete surprise."

"I still don't understand how this plan is going to work,"

Sanders stated more to himself than to the woman on the screen.

"Perform your task and we will take care of the rest," the woman replied, smiling.

"Is he really only now eleven? Has it really only been one year? Christ, he is still just a child," Sanders mumbled.

"Listen, we cannot wait any longer, he is growing suspicious. Please hurry." The video call abruptly ended.

Edmond Sanders sat staring at the video screen in his apartment in Sapphire City for a long while after the conversation ended. It had been more than forty years since he got invited to a birthday party and though he had never been particularly afraid of children, he had no idea what to expect.

Now, sitting alone on a quiet Sunday afternoon, he was going to deliver a birthday cake a boy who had become a hero to every human, both on Earth and on the colonies.

Sanders looked at himself for a moment in the mirror of his apartment as he made the call to order the cake and took a deep breath. "God help me, I'm hopeless."

—

Connor's eleventh birthday party was in full swing on Valhalla Island, a two-acre island two miles off the coast of Sapphire City near the center of Lake Amsvartnir. The waves breaking against the island's rocky shore sprayed the cool mist of the water upward. The house, which was described by the colonists who had seen it as a "temple to a woman's fiery spirit," used the raw energy of the island to emphasize the building's defiance of nature. It was the home of William and Marlena Mercer, known throughout the galaxy as, "The Heroes of the Free Man Revolution."

The children at the party were playing outside; some were

fishing from the dock of the lake, others throwing rocks and talking on the deck that overlooked the water.

"Our own little paradise, to enjoy all alone," William said to himself, taking a deep breath of sweet fresh air.

William Mercer stood by the grill, cooking hamburgers for his guests while wondering to himself, not for the first time, if he was dreaming as his raven-haired wife walked up beside him with a drink in each hand.

"Here is your wine, Mr. Mercer." She kissed him while she handed him the drink.

"Thank you, Mrs. Mercer," William replied, taking a sip and setting the glass down on the table beside him.

They looked at each other for a long while, until Marlena blushed and turned away.

Marlena and William watched a boat skip across the lake and waved as Lyria and her aunt climbed onto the dock.

"Alex should be here any minute," Marlena said, hugging her son's girlfriend.

"No problem, Miss Mercer. Where should I put this?" she asked, holding a wrapped box for Connor.

"Please, it's Marlena. I'll show you, inside," the woman said, leading Lyria into the kitchen.

Alex spent a lot of his downtime in town with Lyria, helping her in the café, and he even started learning guitar to accompany her singing at the amphitheater on Friday nights. William and Marlena had been attending the concerts regularly and enjoyed them immensely.

Marlena returned to William a few minutes later, leaning against the rail and smiling as he cooked.

"Where is Alex anyway?" William asked, flipping a hamburger.

"He had training this morning for a few hours. There

are some new recruits in the volunteer defense militia," she explained.

"Aren't most of the kids from Black Squadron training recruits? He couldn't take the morning off for Connor's birthday?" William retorted.

"Yeah well, you know Alex. He never lets anyone do something he isn't willing to do himself. Besides, I think he wanted to go to his dad's grave today. It's been pretty hard on him," she answered before going back inside to talk to their guests.

Ethan had been given a hero's funeral and was buried on a mountaintop a short flight away. Alex went to the grave often, sometimes taking Connor with him. The two never talked about it much outside of that, though.

A short time later, Skoll landed on the docking pad and Alex got out, meeting Lyria at the door. The boy picked the girl up and spun her in a circle before joining the party. Alex spent most of the day with her and Austin, who had also taken a job training the militia as Alex's second in command.

"Are Pip and Mimelia going to be here?" Marlena asked him within earshot of William.

"No, Mom, remember? They took that job with the new colony expedition team. I think they are on some new planet trying to find a good colony site," Alex said while eating.

"Oh right, I'm surprised they didn't ask you to go." She sat down next to him.

"They did! I want to at some point, but I've been too busy here, and never have the time," Alex said, drawing a frown from Lyria.

"You know, if you want to go explore the galaxy, don't stop on my account," the girl jabbed, playfully.

"I am right where I want to be," Alex answered tactfully.

"She's a lot like you," William said to Marlena, sitting down with his family.

"What, in control?" his wife shot back playfully.

The banter went on for several minutes, followed by laughter as the levity of life on the paradise world of Aeris VII settled in.

—

Connor was inside with his friends from Blue Army laughing at a joke they had between them. Amanda, Tim, Wade, Jinn, Aaron, Marshall, Liam, and Toby stayed close to their old friend, happy to be enjoying his company.

Amanda and Aaron both lived with their families on Aeris VII now and saw Connor fairly often at the school they attended, the others lived on other colonies with their families who survived the war but kept in contact with their OMBI messaging system often. They had all made it out for Connor's birthday party though, none of their families wanting to miss the chance to brush elbows with heroes.

A knock on the door interrupted the friends inside and Connor moved to answer the door. He opened it to see the grinning wolfish face of Edmund Sanders, who had retired from the military to work in a local silver minting shop.

Connor's smile vanished immediately.

"What do you want?" Connor snapped.

"You haven't changed much in a year, have you?" Sanders asked.

Connor shut the door and turned around to walk back to his friends. William laughed as he walked by Connor to let Sanders in.

"Glad you made it," William said, hugging the frowning man.

"I guess the kid doesn't want his cake," Sanders said loudly, walking by a glaring Connor and into the kitchen.

Connor was on his feet in an instant, very much an eleven-year-old boy.

"I was just joking," Connor said harshly, his eyes pleading as he looked at the large box.

Sanders laughed. "It's fine, kid. I think I can let it slide for the savior of the human race."

"Don't call me that," Connor snapped, his eyes on the cake. "I hate it."

"Why?" Sanders asked simply.

"It's stupid," Connor replied just as simply.

As the day went on Connor excitedly opened his presents, throwing the socks that Alex had got him off the deck into the water. Edmund Sanders earned points with Connor when the kid bit into the three-tiered, marbled cake. After three pieces, he sat down on the couch and fell asleep for a while.

As the guests left and night fell on Sapphire City, William and Marlena cleaned up their house, exhausted. Alex, who had been staying in the city most nights, agreed to spend the night on Connor's request and the two went up to their room. As they closed the door, William heard Alex teasing Connor about his crush on Amanda, and smiled.

"Still the same as they ever were," William commented, bringing a cup of steaming tea to Marlena on the couch.

They had the lights off in the house, but with the blinds open and the light reflecting off the water from Sapphire City, the room was illuminated with a soft glow.

The dark-haired woman of unparalleled beauty snuggled up to her husband, vowing never to take a quiet moment with him for granted. Six years of being apart did not dim the fire between them.

"It's like it never happened," she replied, resting her head on William's strong shoulder.

The man put his arm around his wife and held her close, getting slightly choked up, remembering all the nights he had spent missing her, thinking she was gone forever.

There were many such moments in the last few months, William trying to adjust to waking up next to his wife again, comforted in the sound of her breathing while she slept. The reunion was harder than they had expected it to be, only in that there were so many feelings they had buried for so long, that showing them was overwhelming at times.

As the night slipped on they heard Connor's voice upstairs talking softly and smiled at each other.

"He's still a kid and he has the incredible power at his fingertips now. Do you think it's going to be okay?" William asked seriously as Marlena began to fall asleep.

"Yeah, you did so good raising him. I'm sure he will be just fine. Besides, his brother is right there with him, probably keeping him up with war stories."

William was hopeful as he sat awake on the couch, his wife falling asleep in his arms.

"I'm sure you're right," William said softly to his sleeping wife.

—

Alex had fallen asleep almost as soon as they had gotten into their beds and was snoring contently. Connor sat on his bed, whispering quietly to the Omega and Muriel.

"It was fun seeing my friends, I wish they never had to leave," Connor lamented out loud.

"All things end, Initiator," Omega responded in a somber tone.

"But it sucks when it's something good," Connor answered back.

"If things did not end, their value would diminish until they were taken for granted. As old experiences fade, so too are new ones born," Muriel stated whimsically.

"I guess so. Wait, what do you mean? What do you know?" Connor asked, not missing the implicative tone.

—

William was nodding off, listening to his wife's rhythmic breathing, when he noticed Connor at the top of the stairs.

"You okay?" William asked quietly.

In response, Connor's eyes shifted through several visual ranges, illuminating them in different colors.

"She was right," Connor whispered.

"Who was right, about what?" William asked curiously.

"Mom is pregnant," Connor whispered, smiling.

William was silent for a long moment before tears began to rim his dark-blue eyes.

"Are you sure?" William whispered back.

Connor nodded excitedly.

"Muriel says it's a girl," Connor said, looking at the bracer on his right wrist.

"Is that right?" William said as a tear rolled down his cheeks.

"We should name her Nephilim," Connor stated suddenly. "It means, the child of angels and men."

"Yeah, I know. That's a good name, Connor. A very good name."

Connor and William sat grinning at each other in the darkness for a long while, letting the news sink in.

"Thanks for my party. I know you don't like those, but I

had a lot of fun! I'm going back to bed. Goodnight, William," Connor whispered before running back upstairs.

"Goodnight, Connor," William said, long after he was out of earshot.

The man sat quietly for a long time, listening to the waves outside crash against the rocky shore, lost in thought. Eventually, feeling the exhaustion of the day finally catching up with him, he picked up his beautiful, sleeping wife and carried her up to bed.

End

ABOUT THE AUTHOR

 Born on a snowy morning in LaGrande, Oregon, Joseph Mackay was raised with two brothers in Placerville, California. A born adventurer, Joseph has lived in an RV full time and off the back of a motorcycle, has flown a helicopter and enjoyed skydiving. When not writing, he enjoys playing bass guitar, weight lifting, playing with his dog "Mimi," watching Giants baseball, and preparing for his next adventure.

Interested in contacting me?
Please direct all emails to josephmackay@gmail.com

Want to stay current with the latest news and releases?
Check out: www.josephmackaybooks.com

www.ingramcontent.com/pod-product-compliance
Lightning Source LLC
Chambersburg PA
CBHW061145170626
46809CB00003B/987